Also by Graham Reid

BILLY: THREE PLAYS FOR TELEVISION

REMEMBRANCE

GRAHAM REID

faber and faber

LONDON · BOSTON

First published in 1985
by Faber and Faber Limited
3 Queen Square London WC1N 3AU

Filmset by Wilmaset Birkenhead Merseyside
Printed in Great Britain by
Whitstable Litho Ltd Whitstable Kent
All rights reserved

British Library Cataloguing in Publication Data

Reid, J. Graham
Remembrance
I. Title
822'.914 PR6068.E438
ISBN 0–571–13549–8

For Valerie Osborne,
with love and thanks

CHARACTERS

BERT ANDREWS
VICTOR, his son
JENNY, Victor's estranged wife
THERESA DONAGHY
DEIRDRE, elder daughter of Theresa
JOAN, younger daughter of Theresa

Remembrance opened at the Lyric Theatre, Belfast, on 10 October 1984. The cast was as follows:

BERT	Jon Croft
VICTOR	George Shane
THERESA	Doreen Hepburn
DEIRDRE	Frances Quinn
JOAN	Gaylie Runciman
JENNY	Linda Wray

Director	Kevin McHugh
Designer	Edward Lipscomb
Stage Director	Kath Maeso

The play is set in Belfast. The time is the present.

ACT I

SCENE I

The Andrews kitchen. A cluttered table . . . pots, dishes, large empty vodka bottle. BERT *has cleared a space for himself, and is just finishing wrapping a large pile of sandwiches. This done, he starts to fill a very large flask.* VICTOR *enters. He is unshaven, his hair tousled. His shirt is hanging outside his trousers. He wears socks, but no shoes. They greet each other.* BERT *continues his preparations, a little self-consciously now.* VICTOR *stands watching him, lighting a cigarette . . . which action brings on a fierce bout of coughing.* BERT *looks at him disapprovingly.*

BERT: Did you have a party last night?

VICTOR: Dinner party . . . for one.

BERT: I heard you crashing in at God knows what hour. (*Picking up the empty vodka bottle*) I wonder do you have any insides left? (*Packs his flask and sandwiches into a plastic carrier bag.*)

VICTOR: Where are you going?

BERT: The cemetery.

VICTOR: Again. What are you doing up there – digging your own grave?

BERT: It's nice in this good weather.

VICTOR: What's all that stuff for? You don't feed them, do you? (BERT *gives him a disapproving look.*)
There should be a notice: 'Don't feed the corpses.'

BERT: I don't think that's funny. (*Pause.*) I'm tidying up the grave.

VICTOR: Tidying it up . . . you'll be entering that grave for the Chelsea Flower Show before you're finished.

BERT: I notice you don't pay many visits now.

VICTOR: No. Well, I reckon I might be joining him soon enough. So I prefer to spend as much time as possible with the living. Anyway, graveyards don't have the same charm for me that they obviously have for you.

BERT: It's time you pulled yourself together. You're not going to give them many problems if they do come for you.

VICTOR: I've got a broad back . . . can't help that.

11

BERT: If someone was waiting for you, the state you're usually in, you'd be incapable of defending yourself.

VICTOR: You're just afraid they'll have to dig your lovely grave up, to bury me.

BERT: I'm serious, you know.

VICTOR: It would be handy that, for you. Having us all under the one sod.

BERT: Will you bloody well listen to me? I don't want those bastards blowing your brains all over the driveway some night.

VICTOR: I'm not Sam. They'll never find an Andrews off guard again.

BERT: (*Handing him his gun*) That was under the grill.

VICTOR: (*Taking it*) So what's under my pillow?

BERT: Your toast probably. What was it doing under the grill?

VICTOR: I don't know. I must have just set it there when I came in. Proves I had it at the ready.

(BERT *just looks at him.*)

You have to admit that would have fooled them.

BERT: Not half as much as it would have fooled you . . . since you couldn't even remember you'd left it there. (*Pause.*) Could you even manage to use it, if you had to?

VICTOR: Course I could. Don't know if I'd hit you, me, or them . . . but I'd fire the fucker.

(BERT *just shakes his head. Takes the lid off a pot.*)

BERT: What's all this spaghetti doing in here?

VICTOR: I forgot about it.

BERT: (*Agitated*) What do you mean? It's a full pot. How could you forget about it?

VICTOR: I put it on, forgot about it, and opened a tin of soup. By the time I'd had the soup I didn't feel like it. Anyway, it's overcooked. (*Inspects it.*) You could always make golf balls with it.

BERT: Well, you can tidy this mess up. I'm damned if I will.

VICTOR: I'll buy you a dishwasher for Christmas.

BERT: Are you planning to leave it there until Christmas?

VICTOR: Who will you nag at when I go? I'm thinking of emigrating.

BERT: Staying sober would be simpler.

VICTOR: Straight up.

BERT: The moon?

VICTOR: Don't sharpen your wits on my hangover . . . that's hardly cricket. No. South Africa.

BERT: What would you do in South Africa?

VICTOR: (*Aiming his gun at the wall, pretending to shoot*) Good cops are appreciated over there. Kick the black bollocks off the nigs and nobody says 'boo' to you.

BERT: Would you stop playing with that thing? You make me nervous.

VICTOR: Nervous . . . an ex-soldier afraid of a gun?

BERT: We were taught respect . . . to respect our weapon and to respect ourselves. You respect neither.

VICTOR: Thanks, Da. You'll understand if I don't give your name to the South African Government, as a referee.

BERT: You're not going to South Africa.

VICTOR: I've told you, no bull. There's none of this oul nonsense about molesting prisoners over there. Change the television channels here and the bastards are reporting you. Over there you're in trouble if you don't molest them. Appreciation . . . that's all a good cop asks.

BERT: (*Irritated*) You're not a good cop. Christ . . . would you go and take a look at yourself.

VICTOR: (*Rubbing his chin*) Splash of water, and a dig at the grave . . . ooops . . . I'll look as good as new.

BERT: I'm 68 years old. I've fought in a war. I've buried a wife, and a son. But I've never let myself go the way you have. Take a look at yourself.

VICTOR: You're repeating yourself, Da. (*Annoyed at* BERT's *anger*) The wife you buried was my mother and the son you buried was my brother and the scum who murdered him threaten my life every day. (*Pause.*) Shaving every day's not the most important thing in my life.

BERT: Look at the state you have this place in. If you want to live like a pig, find yourself a sty. Don't turn my home into one.

VICTOR: Don't you have my wife in to clean it for you?

13

BERT: Your ex-wife.

VICTOR: Ex-wife, non-wife, call her what you like, she still wipes up after you.

BERT: I pay her for what she does.

VICTOR: You pay her, I pay her, the wee whore does all right.

BERT: That's enough of that talk. Jenny's a good girl. She was lost on you.

VICTOR: Is it not time you went for your date with the dead?

BERT: I remember you when you were full of pride, and self-respect.

VICTOR: All right, Da, will you wrap it up? To you the day might be well advanced but this is my dawn. My head hasn't come to terms with it yet. I don't want a lecture.

BERT: I don't think the job's worth the price you're paying.

VICTOR: Listen. (*Quiet*) I like my job. You mightn't think I'm good at it but I know I am.

BERT: What are you good at, Victor? Bashing suspects around the room? Knocking heads against walls? Is that the job you take so much pride in doing?

VICTOR: (*Angry, but quiet*) When you're at your son's grave today, you think how he died, and who killed him. Take a look around that cemetery. You'll discover he's not on his own. I might bash the odd head on the odd wall but I'll never blow an unarmed man's head off from three feet. You remember when you plant your flowers on the top of that grave, that my brother's underneath the fucker.

(VICTOR *goes.* BERT *stands a moment, shaken. He picks up his bag and leaves.*)

A bench in the cemetery. There is a handbag and a box of pastries sitting on it. THERESA *comes along. She has been waiting for some time and is pacing up and down. Sits. Pause. Looks round and smiles at someone approaching.* BERT *arrives, a little out of breath.*

BERT: Sorry I'm late, love.

THERESA: I was just beginning to get anxious.

BERT: I got into an argument with Victor.

THERESA: You two, what was it this time?

BERT: I suppose what it really is every time . . . us two just being in the same house together.

THERESA: It wasn't too nasty, was it?

BERT: I can cope. I understand Victor, you see. He doesn't think I do, but I do. We talk the same language. I just speak a more standardized version, that's all.

THERESA: I think my Deirdre and him would have a lot in common.

BERT: Yes . . . and they'd have a lot not in common.
(They sit for a moment, enjoying the day.)

THERESA: Isn't it beautiful . . . lovely weather. Listen to the birds. (*Pause.*) I saw a blackbird this morning . . . eating a worm. A disgusting, fat, slimy thing. (*Pulls a face.*) I thought, what a horrible thing to have to have for breakfast . . . so I threw it a bit of currant cake.

BERT: Did it prefer that?

THERESA: It flew away . . . and then came back, for the worm.

BERT: Perhaps it didn't like currants.
(Pause.)

THERESA: Isn't it a shame you have to be dead to get this sort of peace and quiet?

BERT: There's not so many use it now. Cremation's the great thing nowadays.

THERESA: The very thought of it makes me shiver. They'll never get me into one of them furnaces. (*Looking around*) This is where I want to be.

BERT: When you're gone, you're gone, I suppose. You'll be none the wiser.

THERESA: I heard it's a take on. They take the bodies out and save the coffins. Earth burial's the Christian way. A nice service and a nice tea afterwards.

BERT: (*Organizing things*) Talking of tea . . .

THERESA: (*Looking at his flask*) That's a big one you've got.

BERT: What? Oh yes, I like tea. (*Pause.*) Have you heard the joke, about the Irishman who arrived late for a cremation funeral? He rushed in, just as the coffin was disappearing, smashed two eggs on it, threw a bit of bacon on. He shouted, 'Put them through as well, I'd no time for breakfast.' (*He laughs. She doesn't.*)

THERESA: (*With a weak smile*) Oh yes, very good. (*They eat.*)

BERT: You know, I wonder if I was away tomorrow who'd look after this place? Victor wouldn't, that's for sure.

THERESA: The young ones . . . neither of those two ladies of mine'll come near the place. It's Joan's nerves, mind, but Deirdre could come . . . but she wouldn't.

BERT: Maybe it's just as well in a way. After all, we mightn't have got together.

THERESA: The young aren't as thoughtful. (*Pause.*) You notice, there's never very many young ones about.

BERT: It's a working day, I suppose. Anyway, the young think it's morbid. They don't want to be thinking about it. I suppose you don't when you're young.

THERESA: My fella didn't get the choice. (*Crossing herself*) God rest him.

BERT: Come on, eat away at them sandwiches.

THERESA: (*Eating*) That's beautiful cooked ham.

BERT: Didn't I tell you? The best in the city.

THERESA: Did you forget about the mustard?

BERT: Aye. I was in a bit of a rush . . . getting it all ready, before that Victor fella came around.

THERESA: But you didn't . . .
(*He shakes his head.*)
. . . and you forgot the mustard. It's a nice cup of tea, though.

16

BERT: It's not too strong?

THERESA: No, it's grand. I've brought two nice fresh cream doughnuts and some currant cake.

BERT: The blackbird didn't get it all, then?

THERESA: You know, when I saw the size of that worm I shuddered. With this being a graveyard and all, you get to wondering why the worms are so fat.

BERT: You can get fat worms anywhere.

THERESA: They're all fat here, though. It makes my skin crawl.

BERT: You don't get that with cremation.

THERESA: Do you want to be cremated?

BERT: It's cheaper, so I don't suppose I'll have much choice with that Victor fella.

THERESA: Surely with all the overtime the polis get, he can afford to give you a decent burial?

BERT: Anyway (*looking at her*) maybe it'll not be his responsibility.
(*She looks at him shyly.*)

THERESA: Do you think him and his wife'll ever get together again?

BERT: I doubt it. I doubt if Jenny'd be interested. Not in the state he's in at the moment. He's a mess.

THERESA: It's the strain, I suppose. The fear . . . and the strain.

BERT: It's the drink.

THERESA: That's because of the strain and fear. My man was the same. He lived in fear of someone offering him a job. (*Crossing herself*) God forgive me for speaking ill of the dead, but he was a terrible man and you daren't have looked sideways at him when he'd a drop taken. Many a clout I got. For a couple of years before he died, I barely knew what it was like to see out of both eyes together.

BERT: It must have had a very bad effect on the children.

THERESA: It did. Peter always swore he'd never drink when he got married . . . but sure . . . He was engaged, you know. He'd been up seeing her that night . . . must have decided to take a short cut home. It was a short cut to here.

BERT: Did they shoot him?

THERESA: (*Emotional*) Eventually they did him that kindness.

BERT: (*Touching her hand*) I remember this used to be the safest city in Europe. You could have walked anywhere. Many's the time I was the last bus into Short Strand. I'd walk home, up through the markets, along Donegall Pass.

THERESA: His wee girl used to come up to see me, ach for months afterwards. She was heartbroken, until she met somebody else. She's married now, has a couple of youngsters. I don't mind that – you can't mourn your whole life – but he was a friend of Peter's. I thought that was a bit much.

BERT: Isn't it strange, we were here together that morning, a few hundred yards apart, burying our sons.

THERESA: Come on, this cooked ham's too good to be morbid over. Could I have a drop more tea?

BERT: Sure, sure, hold steady. (*Refills both their cups.*) That sun's strong. (*Removes his pullover.*) I'm boiled.

THERESA: Be careful now. Summer chills can be treacherous.

BERT: I'd hate to be a gravedigger in weather like this. The ground hard . . . digging, sweating.

THERESA: I'd hate to be a gravedigger in any weather. Mind you, it must be worse for the cremators, weather like this. No wonder you never see a fat gravedigger.

BERT: I suppose now, with all this equality, we'll have women doing it soon.

THERESA: If I was going to be equal to men, I'd rather be equal to something better than a gravedigger.

BERT: Look . . . there's a couple over there. Skinny, that one on the left, you can barely see him behind the shaft of his spade.

THERESA: Why do they wear those big belts and braces? I suppose, right enough, it wouldn't do if your trousers dropped in the middle of a funeral.

BERT: I think those belts are to prevent back strain . . . all the stooping and digging.

THERESA: Huh, I wouldn't have given gravediggers credit for having that much wit.

BERT: I don't know. There was a taxi driver once won *Mastermind*.

THERESA: He was a Cockney, though. They're a real crafty lot them. Did you ever see that one who throws darts? I've never seen anybody as sly-looking as thon . . . and that finger, the way it sticks out . . . you couldn't trust a man like that.

BERT: Do you think he would make a good gravedigger?

THERESA: You'd be hard pushed to find belts to go round the beer-bellies of the half of those fellas. Aren't they revolting? Nearly as bad as those pasty-faced, bleary-eyed snooker players. I thought sport was supposed to be a healthy thing?

BERT: I like snooker. (*Pause.*) Are we being foolish, Theresa, I mean, at our ages?

THERESA: I suppose to some it'll seem that way. I don't feel foolish. Or if that is what I feel, I like feeling foolish.

BERT: We can't go on meeting here every day.

THERESA: Well, either we stop meeting . . . or we meet somewhere else.

BERT: Your place or mine?

THERESA: We're old enough to please ourselves.

BERT: That Victor fella . . . well, he's a bit bigoted, I suppose.

THERESA: He'll make a match for that eldest one of mine, then. You'd expect that, in an RUC man. They must live on their nerves. There've been that many of them shot.

BERT: I'd like to bring you home. If I thought he was out.

THERESA: Bert, your Victor doesn't frighten me – and I think I'm a bit old for hiding around corners.

BERT: I don't want him offending you. I don't want any sort of unpleasantness.

THERESA: Is he with you for good?

BERT: It's beginning to look that way.

THERESA: We could always go to the pictures.

BERT: Would you like to?

THERESA: Yes, but not every night – and the days of short walks and long stands up entries are well behind me.

BERT: We could try it – going home, I mean.

THERESA: You could always come to my place.

BERT: Well, yes, yes . . . What about your daughters?

THERESA: What about them?

BERT: You said the eldest one was . . . bitter.

THERESA: You're a big lad, I'm sure you can look after yourself. If I'm not frightened of your monster, there's no reason why you should be frightened of mine.

BERT: Except you've got two.

THERESA: Joan's no problem. I sometimes wish she was.

The Donaghy living room. JOAN *sits. She wears an apron. She is cleaning brasses.* DEIRDRE *enters. They greet each other.*

DEIRDRE: You're going to have those brasses rubbed away before you're done.

JOAN: Where are the children?

DEIRDRE: At school . . . summer playscheme. Where's my ma?

JOAN: She went up to the cemetery.

DEIRDRE: It's not healthy the way you two live. She has that grave like a well-kept window box and you've the house like an operating theatre. A wee bit of dirt's human, you know, shows a place is lived in.

JOAN: How do you know what the grave looks like? You never go up.

DEIRDRE: I can guess. (*Laughs.*) Unless she doesn't go to the grave at all.

JOAN: ???

DEIRDRE: Maybe she's having an affair with a gravedigger, eh?

JOAN: Are you visiting Joe today?

DEIRDRE: I'd better, otherwise the bastards won't give me any money.

JOAN: If you were a Protestant you could divorce him.

DEIRDRE: If I was a Protestant, I wouldn't have married him in the first place.

JOAN: You shouldn't have married him anyway. I never liked him.

DEIRDRE: It's a pity about you. I didn't care what you thought. It was love. He swept me off my feet.

JOAN: I think you were in love with the idea of being in love. I never knew anybody as desperate to get married.

DEIRDRE: I'd all these soft notions – me, the contented little home-maker, him out knocking his pan in to keep me in a befitting style. The lazy frigger couldn't have worked to keep himself warm – and mine was the only pan he knocked in.

JOAN: According to the *Belfast Telegraph*, divorce here is on the increase. They took a poll amongst their readers.

DEIRDRE: No wonder then. Reading the *Belfast Telegraph*'s enough to break up any marriage. Have you ever screwed, Joan?

JOAN: ???

DEIRDRE: You know . . . had sex?

JOAN: I know what it means. What's it got to do with you?

DEIRDRE: I'd love a man. What am I supposed to do for the rest of my life?

JOAN: He'll maybe get out. Maybe there'll be an amnesty.

DEIRDRE: I don't want him though. For Christ's sake don't say any of this to my ma. (*Pause.*) Maybe it's just this hot weather. They watch me, you know.

JOAN: Who does?

DEIRDRE: His mates. The women of Ireland must not be enjoying themselves – when their men are serving time for the cause. (*Pause. Upset*) I think I'm going mad.

JOAN: Why don't you put the teapot on?

DEIRDRE: I'm sexually frustrated, emotionally deprived, severely depressed – not thirsty.

JOAN: You need a holiday.

DEIRDRE: Thanks, Joan. You've been a great help.

JOAN: Sorry . . .

DEIRDRE: Life has to have more for me than this. I'll be an old woman by the time he gets out. I want a life. I deserve a life.

JOAN: You've the children.

DEIRDRE: Oh yes, great. Five, six and seven. As close together as the bastard could put them. Only for the RUC, I'd probably be the mother of seven, with an eighth on the way.

JOAN: I thought you loved the kids.

DEIRDRE: (*Shouting*) Of course I love the fucking kids. (*Pause.*) Sorry, sorry, love. (*Pause.*) The latest in birth control – a three a.m. arrest, and a life sentence. Now some well-meaning idiots want to let them screw us at visiting time – marvellous.

JOAN: Do you talk to Joe about it?

DEIRDRE: I don't talk to Joe about anything. I listen to Joe, about Joe. You know it's not really the man who serves the life sentence. Christ, sometimes I think capital punishment wouldn't be a bad thing. At least we'd be free to start again. (*Pause.*) Put that teapot on, love, will you?

JOAN: (*Looking at her, concerned*) Sit down . . . relax . . . it'll not take a minute. You should see the doctor.

DEIRDRE: Yes, even he'd do – anything in trousers. (*Pause.*) Sometimes I think I've woken up in the wrong lifetime. I should go back to being a dog, or a frog, or whatever I was before. Mind you, with my luck, I was probably Dr Crippen's wife. (*Pause.*) I woke up feeling very randy this morning.

(JOAN *looks disapprovingly.*)

Don't look at me like that. You just don't realize. Nobody does. The kids were kicking up a racket, and I wanted to hear a man's voice telling them to behave. I wanted to reach an arm out and touch someone.

JOAN: Don't you think it's hard for him too?

DEIRDRE: Yes, of course. We should never forget the guilty.

JOAN: I thought you believed in all of that?

DEIRDRE: Today I believe in me. Mother Ireland will have to take a back seat.

JOAN: I promised you tea.

DEIRDRE: Yes – as a substitute for all that's missing in my life.

JOAN: There's some bread, brown or white. Men we don't supply.

DEIRDRE: Talking of which, when are you going to . . . ?

JOAN: Don't. I claim one day free from the 'you need a nice young man' routine.

DEIRDRE: A 'nice' young man's the last thing you need. He'd probably sit helping you to clean those damned brasses.

JOAN: It's good therapy. I need to be doing something.

DEIRDRE: We're all in the same boat, aren't we? I mean life is a life sentence, isn't it? Don't you think so? I mean hobbies, chores, duties, responsibilities – they're all ways of helping us get through a life sentence, aren't they?

JOAN: (*Pondering*) No . . . maybe . . . yes, and yes.

DEIRDRE: I don't know why, with your decisiveness, your life's fell apart. (*Pause.*) I'm sorry. Oh Christ, what am I doing? I'm a mess, Joan. It's one of those days. Every so often I realize the significance of that emptiness on the other side of the bed.

(JOAN *looks at her sympathetically. Then goes to make the tea.*)

SCENE 4

The cemetery. THERESA *and* BERT *eating doughnuts.*

BERT: These things must be fattening.

THERESA: (*Shocked*) I didn't realize.

BERT: It's the cream.

THERESA: I didn't realize your young fella'd been murdered. There's me going on about Peter . . .

BERT: I'd rather talk about the doughnuts.

THERESA: It's no wonder Victor's so bitter.

BERT: Or the weather. It's bloody hot.

THERESA: (*Looking at him*) You haven't tried the currant cake.

BERT: I'll have it later.

THERESA: Later – how long are we staying here for?

BERT: What is there to rush away for?

THERESA: I'd like to talk about it, Bert. We've really got something in common. Did the ones who did it own up?

BERT: Yes. They sent a postcard, 'Greetings from Hell. Wish you were here.' And I was. (*Pause. Emotional*) . . . sorry.

THERESA: (*Takes his hand.*) Oh, Bert . . . Bert . . . I know . . . I know.
(*They look at each other for a moment. Then kiss, for the first time ever. Break apart, embarrassed. Pause. Both facing front.*)

BERT: I suppose this weather can't really last much longer.

THERESA: We'll have a water shortage soon. A few days' good weather and we have a water shortage.

BERT: It's a storage problem.

THERESA: If you ask me, it's an intelligence problem. I think it's all that tea them Civil Servants drink causes it.

BERT: I wouldn't want to stop coming here – especially when the weather's fine like this.

THERESA: They keep this one nice. I like a well-kept cemetery.

BERT: I don't mind very old ones being overgrown.
(*Pause. They sit for a moment, then look at each other and smile.*)

THERESA: I'm always giving off when I see young ones snogging in the street.

BERT: It isn't quite the street.

THERESA: Some people might say it's even worse. I haven't been kissed like that since I was courting my husband.

BERT: I was always a good kisser.

THERESA: (*Good-natured*) I meant outside.

BERT: Elsie was terrible about that, always. Holding hands was as far as she'd go, in public.

THERESA: I liked a kiss or two, the occasional ear-nibble. Mind you, I had to be careful. If he'd had a few drinks he'd have bitten the ear off me. He was never really romantic. He was an awkward man. If he was sober, you knew twenty minutes beforehand that he was working up to a kiss. By the time it actually came the notion had gone of me.

BERT: Even up until near the end Elsie got annoyed – if I kissed her in front of the other patients.

THERESA: Did she linger long?

BERT: She was sick for years . . . a lot of pain. I could never believe it was part of a grand design. Mind you, she had great faith. Until the very end.

THERESA: He went in the street. His brother had a coal business. He was giving him a hand out, one cold November Wednesday. He had the bag on his back and all. Half-way across the road and down he went, bag and all, dead. Mind you, that Sean one wasn't too far gone with grief that he didn't shovel up every last bit of coal. (*Pause.*)

BERT: You never know how you're going to react. People do strange things. The night Sam was shot on our drive, we ran out, I kicked over the milk bottles and Victor stopped to pick them up. Reflex, I suppose.

THERESA: He was a stubborn man, Joe, awful stubborn. Wouldn't go near the doctor about the pains in his chest. I think he was just afraid of being told to give up the drink. Still, maybe it's not a bad way to go.
(*Pause.*) There are worse wastes, when you look around you, today.

26

(Pause. Both sit, gloomy.)

BERT: Would you like to come home with me?

THERESA: Today?

BERT: No, tomorrow, tomorrow night.

THERESA: Oh dear, the thought of meeting children's even more frightening than the thought of meeting parents. Will Victor be there?

BERT: It's my house.

THERESA: Owning the kennel doesn't stop your dog from biting.

BERT: Come on, we'll be a long time in a place like this.

(They sit quietly sipping their tea. Each thinking about the visit.)

SCENE 5

The Andrews kitchen. JENNY *is there. She has it almost tidied.*
VICTOR *comes in. He is now clean and dressed. He stands for a*
moment, watching her. She is self-conscious, but pretends not to
notice him. When he speaks she pretends to be startled.

VICTOR: Sorry about the mess.

JENNY: I didn't see you there.

VICTOR: I gave a supper party last night.

JENNY: Lovely.

VICTOR: The spaghetti didn't go down very well. Did you throw
    it out?

JENNY: No, it's there.

VICTOR: I was thinking . . . you could knit me a bullet-proof
    vest with it.

JENNY: I thought you'd gone to work.

VICTOR: They sent me back to keep an eye on you. You're a
    suspect . . . a security risk . . . the company you keep.
    (*Pause. She refuses to be drawn.*)
    Do you like cleaning up after me and my da?

JENNY: The money helps.

VICTOR: I'd have thought you'd have plenty of money – given
    your friend's connections.

JENNY: Victor, please don't start all this again. I don't see him
    now, you know that.

VICTOR: Bit embarrassing for me. My ex-wife involved with one
    of the country's biggest terrorists.

JENNY: If you're going to start this, I'm going home.

VICTOR: Suit yourself. I'll see to it you don't get paid.

JENNY: I don't see him any more. As soon as I knew about him
    I stopped.

VICTOR: Not before he'd got all he wanted from you, I'm sure.
    It was a great laugh for them – at my expense. I'll get that
    bastard though.

JENNY: Get him – why?

VICTOR: For fucking my wife.

28

JENNY: Don't you dare speak to me like that. (*Pause*.) There was nothing like that. It was just friendship. As soon as I discovered he was married I stopped. I wasn't going to do to another woman what had been done to me.

VICTOR: I see, so it wasn't because of the risk to me?

JENNY: Nothing I do will increase the risk to you. Anyway, he's not in the IRA.

VICTOR: You were never very fussy about the company you kept.

JENNY: You're the living proof of that.

VICTOR: Well, then, you'll be pleased to know. I'm emigrating.

JENNY: Where to? When?

VICTOR: I admire your self-control. The way you carefully disguise your enthusiasm. South Africa. Soon.

JENNY: Are you serious?

VICTOR: Time I moved on.

JENNY: Why South Africa?

VICTOR: The laws there suit my temperament.

(JENNY *finds this side of* VICTOR *distasteful, and her look says so.*)

JENNY: Will I throw out this spaghetti?

VICTOR: Have it for lunch if you like.

JENNY: I don't like spaghetti. It reminds me of worms.

VICTOR: Do you want a divorce?

JENNY: If I say yes, do I have to eat this spaghetti?

VICTOR: You'd be free then to flirt with your paramilitary godfathers.

JENNY: I don't need a divorce to be free to choose my company. You're the one who broke faith in our marriage. I never looked at another man when we were together.

VICTOR: The trouble was, sometimes you didn't even look at me.

JENNY: A lot of the time you weren't very attractive to look at.

VICTOR: You never understood the pressures I was under.

JENNY: I think I did. I just didn't see that as a justification for sleeping with other women.

VICTOR: Just a view of life. I could go tomorrow – so what do I save myself for?

29

JENNY: Fine. Well, that's the point we're at now.

VICTOR: And are you happy?

JENNY: No, but I'm not frightened in the same way.

VICTOR: Would you consider having another go?

JENNY: I'd rather not have this conversation.

VICTOR: No court of appeal with you?

JENNY: I've cut my losses, Victor. I might never really be happy again – but I'll settle for not being any more miserable than I am now.

VICTOR: I never beat you. You always had enough money.

JENNY: You did beat me. Not with your fists. With your presence. With our marriage.

VICTOR: What sort of shit is this? Beat you with our marriage! If people heard you talking like that they'd laugh at you.

JENNY: You know what I'm talking about. Don't try to fool me with your 'thick peeler's' routine. That's the thing I dislike most about you. This attempt to portray yourself as a working-class thickie.

VICTOR: I am working class.

JENNY: You've had an education. You're an intelligent or at least a well-educated man. That job has destroyed you. I don't think you're doing Sam – or the memory of Sam – any good by pretending to be an unthinking fascist thug. I used to respect you and that helped me to live with the risks, the fears, because I knew you believed in what you were doing and that you were doing it well.

VICTOR: I'm going in here to watch the racing. I've a few bets on.

JENNY: When I met you, you didn't know one end of a racehorse from another.

VICTOR: So living with you was educational.

JENNY: (*Moving towards him*) Victor . . .

VICTOR: (Fiercely) Fuck off. Just fuck off.

(*He goes.*)

The Andrews living room. BERT *and* THERESA *sitting with tea and biscuits. They are a little uneasy. She hasn't been there long.*

THERESA: Is it a warm house?

BERT: Yes . . . once it warms up. We have the central heating.

THERESA: I'd be ashamed to bring you to mine, after seeing this.

BERT: Don't be silly. I've done a lot of work on it.

THERESA: Did you put the heating in yourself?

BERT: Yes . . . Sam and me.

THERESA: That one of mine, he'd hardly have put a shovel of coal on, let alone put central heating in.

BERT: I just happen to like DIY . . .

THERESA: So did he. That's all I ever got. Ask him to do something – 'do it yourself.'

BERT: Is that tea all right?

THERESA: Fine, lovely.

BERT: Sorry the biscuits aren't more exciting.

THERESA: They're fine, lovely.

BERT: I feel a bit silly really. I'd like . . . would you like. . . ?

THERESA: (*Holding out her cup*) Yes, please.

BERT: (*Taking it*) Oh, aye, right.
  (*Obviously not what he had in mind. He goes.*)

THERESA: (*Calling to him, off*) Could I have just a half-spoonful of sugar this time?

BERT: (*Off*) I didn't know you took sugar.

THERESA: I don't, except now and again. Just a half-spoon.

BERT: (*Returning with her tea*) You should have said before.

THERESA: It's all right. Really.
  (*They sit.* BERT *glancing at her from time to time, trying to think of something to say.*)

BERT: It needs redecorating, this place.

THERESA: Gracious, if you think this needs redecorating, I dread to think what you'll say about mine. He didn't believe in redecorating until the wallpaper pattern started fading.

BERT: I suppose it takes all kinds.

THERESA: You can say that again. (*Pause.*) Mind you, I missed him.

(BERT *gropes and finds her hand, without looking round.*)

BERT: Are you warm enough?

THERESA: (*Looking at his hand, amused by his embarrassment*) I'm hoping to be. (*They face each other and kiss tentatively, then more passionately, but not greatly so. They spring apart when the outside door bangs.* VICTOR *enters.* BERT *and* THERESA *are acutely embarrassed.* VICTOR *looks at them, increasing their embarrassment and aware he's doing so.*)

VICTOR: Sorry I'm early.

BERT: (*Rising*) Victor, this, ah . . . this is . . . Mrs . . . Theresa . . .

VICTOR: (*Taking her hand*) Mrs Theresa. Do you mean Mother Theresa, Da?

THERESA: How do you do, Victor?

VICTOR: I was going to ask you how things were in Calcutta. Are you related?

THERESA: Pardon?

VICTOR: To Mother Theresa?

THERESA: (*Uneasy*) No . . . not that I know of.

BERT: I didn't expect you home so early.

VICTOR: Obviously. Well, I decided to stop drinking . . . for tonight. Make a fresh start on it tomorrow. Do you drink, Theresa?

THERESA: Very little. Christmas, weddings, that sort of thing.

VICTOR: Funny how weddings start people drinking. Mine certainly started me.

BERT: There's some tea in the pot.

VICTOR: That's very civil of you, Da. (*Sitting*) Two sugar, and just a little milk. Ta.

(BERT *hesitates, then goes.*)

Do you come here often?

THERESA: No . . . no. This is the first time.

VICTOR: Really. What do you think of it?

THERESA: It's lovely. Very nice.

VICTOR: Yes. My wife – ex-wife – cleans it. My da pays her,

of course. I'm not sure how I feel about that. She's still quite attractive, you see. Sometimes she bends over, you know the way some women do when they're cleaning, without bending her knees. I get such an urge to ride her again.

(THERESA *is shocked*.)

Yes, tragic, isn't it?

(BERT *comes in, aware of* THERESA's *embarrassment but not its cause*.)

'Course, the real tragedy is that she won't let me.

BERT: I hope that's warm enough . . .

VICTOR: Thank you, Da. (*Pause. Drinks*.) Where did you two meet?

THERESA: (*Looking at* BERT) The cemetery . . .

VICTOR: I see. So you're the reason for all the sandwiches and flasks of tea. That's a relief. I was beginning to think my da was planning to open a café for Resurrection Day.

BERT: Victor's got a funny sense of humour, Theresa.

VICTOR: No sense of humour at all, in fact. It's my job, very depressing.

THERESA: I can imagine. You're a policeman?

VICTOR: A torturer, actually. That's why I'm exhausted tonight. Do you know, I've spent the whole day trying to coax a prisoner to jump out through the window? But the ungrateful bastard wouldn't jump. We haven't had a suicide for months. It implies our methods don't work. We're way behind some of the top British police forces. Don't get me wrong, Theresa. I'm totally impartial about it. To me they're all human beings, regardless of religion.

BERT: I think you talk more sense when you're drunk.

THERESA: It must be a terrible job.

VICTOR: Must it? No . . . I like it. I enjoy it.

BERT: Victor, give it a rest.

VICTOR: My da doesn't really understand. You lot read the papers, listen to the news. What is a statistic to you is a shortening of the odds to me.

BERT: We all know about the risks.

VICTOR: What sort of odds do you reckon the bookies would

give me against me ever reaching retirement age, eh?

BERT: Victor's thinking of emigrating, Theresa. He's thinking of going to South Africa.

THERESA: Oh, that'll be nice. Are you going soon?

VICTOR: A great country for policemen, Theresa. You see, out there it doesn't matter if the criminals are Catholic, or Protestant – so long as they're black.

BERT: Victor would like everybody to think he's a bigot.

VICTOR: And of course I'm not. I just hate criminals, niggers and Fenians.

BERT: (*Angry*) Now that's enough. Don't you dare insult Theresa in front of me.

VICTOR: Well, you're excused, if you want to leave the room.

BERT: Now listen you. This is my house.

THERESA: It's all right, Bert. I'm not shocked, or appalled, or insulted – I'm just sad. I think your tragedy is, son, that you'd like to be all the things you say you are and you can't.

BERT: (*As* VICTOR *rises to go*) If you're going to bed, you'd better move your car so I can get out.

VICTOR: (*Throwing his keys to* BERT) Use mine. With any luck it'll be booby-trapped.

(VICTOR *goes.* BERT *and* THERESA *sit, stunned.*)

The Donaghy home. The backyard. JOAN *is sweeping,* THERESA
holding the shovel and putting the dirt into the bin.

THERESA: This weather's gorgeous. Away in and bring two
   chairs out, and we'll sit for a while.

   (*As* JOAN *does so,* THERESA *moves the dustbin across the yard.*
   JOAN *returns and places the chairs.* THERESA *adjusts hers to
   get the best angle. They sit.*)

JOAN: Are you not going to the cemetery today?

THERESA: Not today.

JOAN: Are the flowers up?

THERESA: Yes. It looks a treat.

JOAN: We should have had him cremated and scattered the
   ashes here.

THERESA: Here – in the backyard?

JOAN: He loved it here. Didn't he spend hours out here with his
   pigeons?

THERESA: I saw that one again the other day. I'm sure it was
   one of Peter's.

JOAN: It wouldn't still be coming. Not now the shed's down.
   Sure most pigeons look alike.

THERESA: He knew them all – by name.

JOAN: I'd like to whitewash this place, cover up those marks
   where his shed was.

THERESA: Whitewash gets that dirty after a while.

JOAN: Paint it, then.

THERESA: At the price of paint? We could do with a bit of
   cement between some of those bricks.

JOAN: Pointing, that's called. Putting cement between the
   bricks. That's called pointing.

THERESA: You should have been a bricklayer, love.

JOAN: (*Basking a moment*) Here, Ma, if we get a tan where'll we
   say we were?

THERESA: On the Costa del Sewer. (*Pause.*) Do you think we
   should put in for a move?

35

JOAN: No, I do not.

THERESA: Get a nice house with a garden. We could sunbathe properly then.

JOAN: Right enough – with the youngsters playing football all over the place and the dogs pissing on the fence and shitting all over the garden.

THERESA: Joan, what sort of language is that?

JOAN: Descriptive, I think it's called.

THERESA: Well, find some other way of describing it and don't be so coarse.

JOAN: I'd hate to move away from here.

THERESA: Central heating and all. (*Pause.*) I think we should change.

JOAN: Housing estates are desperate.

THERESA: Break out . . . new things . . . different things.

JOAN: The rent goes up, your consumption of valium goes up.

THERESA: You take more valium than I do.

JOAN: Look at that place where our Deirdre lives.

THERESA: There are nicer places. (*Pause.*) I'd like a nice modern sort of house. A place I'd be proud to bring people into.

JOAN: What people?

THERESA: Any people . . . people I liked . . . friends. I mean, look at this place – A stinking old outside toilet – it's primitive. I'd feel ashamed if a stranger wanted to use that.

JOAN: What are we going to have strangers in the toilet for? It's not what you'd call a tourist attraction.

THERESA: A nice clean working kitchen.

JOAN: Ma, our kitchen is clean. I spend most of my life cleaning it.

THERESA: That's unhealthy too.

JOAN: Cleaning the kitchen's unhealthy?

THERESA: You should be out working – enjoying yourself.

JOAN: Can you do the both together?

THERESA: Be serious, Joan. What would you think if you brought a boyfriend home and he had to use that toilet?

JOAN: ??? That he shit and pissed like the rest of us.

THERESA: Will you stop talking like that, you filthy article.

JOAN: Ma, I don't have a boyfriend.

THERESA: Well, you should have. It's not healthy.

JOAN: What do I want with a boyfriend?

THERESA: (*Looking at her*) What does anybody want with a boyfriend?

JOAN: Do you want me to be crude again?

THERESA: Don't you like boys?

JOAN: Boys are fine but at my age it would have to be a man – and I can't be bothered.

THERESA: A woman needs a man.

JOAN: ???

THERESA: And a man needs a woman. (*Pause.*) It's a need.

JOAN: I'm not queer, if that's what you're thinking.

THERESA: It's a bit odd, not to like men.

JOAN: I didn't say I didn't like them. I find the milkman very pleasant. On the odd occasion we get letters, the postman seems quite nice. Mind you, I'm not so fussed on the coalman, that black face and hands . . .

THERESA: You're not a racialist, are you?

JOAN: They don't have to be white, but I would like them clean.

THERESA: You shouldn't hold the colour of a person's skin against them.

JOAN: I don't.

THERESA: Or their religion.

JOAN: ???

THERESA: I hate bigotry. It doesn't solve any of our problems. (*Pause.*) I know Protestants killed our Peter. I know that. But I don't hate Protestants. (*Pause.*) Hating's not going to bring Peter back. (*Pause.*) Innocent people have died on both sides. There are Protestants like us, who've lost an innocent son – or brother. It's not all on one side, that's all I'm saying.
(*Pause.* THERESA *is aware that* JOAN *has remained silent. She glances at her, puzzled.*)
Do you think I'm talking rubbish?

JOAN: I don't know what you're talking . . . I don't know what this is all about. You've never said things like this before.

THERESA: Do you like Protestants?

JOAN: I hate the people who killed our Peter.

THERESA: But you don't just hate all Protestants?

JOAN: I don't know. It could have been any of them. Until we find out, until they're caught, yes, I suppose I do hate them all.

THERESA: Suppose you met someone in our situation, a Protestant, who'd suffered just the way we have. How would you feel?

JOAN: I don't know. Ma, what's this all about?

THERESA: Bitterness eats away at people. It destroys them. It . . .

JOAN: So does grief.

THERESA: I'm not saying we shouldn't mourn . . . or . . . or . . . we shouldn't . . . or that we should like the people who actually did it. I'm not saying that. All I'm saying is . . . is . . . (*Pause. Then at a great rush*) I met a man in the cemetery, his son was murdered, his wife's dead, he's a Protestant. His other son's a policeman, and I think I'm falling in love with him.

JOAN: With the policeman?

(JOAN *looks at her, dumbfounded.*)

THERESA: Not . . . no . . . with the father . . . the man. (*Looking at* JOAN) Jesus, Mary and Joseph, what have I said?

JOAN: You mean you weren't going to Peter's grave at all?

THERESA: What?

JOAN: All those visits, all this time, I've felt so sorry for you. I've thought you couldn't cope. You've been going up there to see a man. (*Pause. Comprehending*) Is that who the toilet's not good enough for? The kitchen not clean enough for? That's what it's all been about?

THERESA: No. You've taken it up wrong. That's not . . . (*Pause.*)
Don't look at me like that. I haven't committed a crime.

JOAN: Haven't you?

(DEIRDRE *enters. She realizes something is wrong and doesn't know what to say.*)
Deirdre, do you like Protestants?

38

DEIRDRE: Course I do. I'm having one grilled for my dinner.

THERESA: I don't think that's funny, Deirdre. You're the mother of young children. There's enough bitterness around without you teaching it to your children.

DEIRDRE: Have you two been converted or something? Have you seen the Virgin Mary's face in the bricks of the shithouse wall or something?

THERESA: We're trying to have a serious conversation.

JOAN: Really. I was hoping you'd say you weren't serious.

DEIRDRE: Sorry. Will I come back later?

THERESA: Don't be silly. Get yourself a chair and sit down.

JOAN: (*Rising*) She can have mine. (*Glancing at* THERESA) I'm going to tidy the kitchen – in case we have visitors. (*She goes.*)

DEIRDRE: (*Watching her go*) What visitors?

THERESA: Nobody. It's just Joan having a joke.

DEIRDRE: Excuse me for asking, but if that's the way she looks when she's joking, how do we know when she's being serious? (*Pause.*) Have you two had a row?

THERESA: No, no. We're just sitting here enjoying the sun. We got talking that's all.

DEIRDRE: I see, talking. And she's gone to clean the kitchen? The floor's that shiny Torvill and Dean could skate on it.

THERESA: I wish she'd stop this eternal scrubbing and cleaning. It's getting me down. I thought I was getting somewhere, just getting her to sit down and relax with me.

DEIRDRE: Your 'serious conversation' must have been about the wrong things. (*Pause.*) Well, if I'm supposed to know, I'm sure you'll tell me.

THERESA: How're Joe and the kids?

DEIRDRE: Same. He's still imprisoned, they're still impossible – and I'm going fucking mad.

THERESA: Deirdre! For goodness sake. That one next door listens to everything. What's wrong with you?

DEIRDRE: I've told you, but you only heard the bad word. I picked a fight with that whore next door to me last night – just to get somebody to shout at.

THERESA: I've told you to watch her. They're a rough crowd . . .

DEIRDRE: She thought the same and it cost her two teeth.

THERESA: (*Appalled*) What! You mean you actually brawled? In the street?

DEIRDRE: (*Acting it out*) She took a lunge at me. I near shit, but I grabbed her by that peroxide hair of hers and dragged her off her feet.

(THERESA *gapes*.)

Then I hit her a kick on the mouth. (*Holding up her foot*) That's a blood stain.

THERESA: You did what? You actually kicked her? A defenceless woman, lying on the ground, and you lifted your foot and kicked her? In the name of God, what sort of a daughter have I reared?

DEIRDRE: When I think of the abuse I've took from that oul whore, for years, because I was afraid of her. Imagine, me afraid of thon? She was easy.

(THERESA *gives her a look*.)

I felt great afterwards.

THERESA: ???

DEIRDRE: I know now why Joe used to beat me. I think in future, when I'm fed up and frustrated, I'll go in next door and beat the shite out of her.

THERESA: Look, love, I know it's difficult without a man – you don't have to tell me.

DEIRDRE: I think I'll take a lover.

THERESA: Well, I suppose that would be understandable – in the circumstances.

DEIRDRE: (*Amazed*) Did you hear what I said? A lover . . . in bed . . . sex . . . all that nasty stuff.

THERESA: Yes, I heard.

DEIRDRE: (*Touching her*) Are you sure you're my ma? It's not just your body taken over by an alien intelligence, is it?

THERESA: Well, he didn't think of you when he did it, did he?

DEIRDRE: You know, I think he probably did. How else could he have worked up enough anger to kill somebody?

(*Pause.* THERESA *starts removing some pegs from the clothes line*.)

THERESA: Well, I'd expect you to feel the same for me – if I took a lover.

(DEIRDRE *looks at her and starts to laugh.*)

DEIRDRE: You – a lover?

THERESA: I've been a widow for years. What's wrong with that? Will you stop laughing – I didn't crack a joke.

DEIRDRE: Ma, you're in your sixties. Where would you find a lover? In an antique shop?

THERESA: (*Angry*) Away in and make a cup of tea. Do something useful instead of sitting there laughing like a fool.

DEIRDRE: (*Stopping laughing, gazing at* THERESA, *who becomes self-conscious*) Ma, hey, you're not serious, are you? I mean, you don't have a lover, do you?

THERESA: (*Flustered*) No, no, of course not. (*Pause. Aware of* DEIRDRE'*s scrutiny*) You can put your big eyes back in. Of course I haven't got a lover. (*Pause.*) At my age, chance would be a fine thing.

SCENE 8

The Andrews living room. BERT *is reading the morning paper.*
JENNY *comes in.*

JENNY: That's me finished. Are you sure you wouldn't like me
to make you a bit of lunch before I go?

BERT: No, love. I'll probably wait until Victor rises. (*Pause.*)
Jenny . . . I'm very worried about him. This bigot act of
his is getting out of hand.

JENNY: It's his job, this place, drink, Sam's death. (*Pause.*) It's
odd really, I think Sam was always more bigoted than
Victor.

BERT: Sam? Bigoted? Sure, Sam never bothered anybody. He
was innocent.

JENNY: He didn't deserve to be gunned down, but he wasn't a
knight in shining armour. He was no saint. They used to
argue about it. Sam was anti-Catholic, anti-Black,
anti-trades unions. He was very prejudiced, you know that.

BERT: (*Annoyed with her*) My son was the innocent victim of
murdering bastards . . . scum . . .

JENNY: Don't get upset. I've said he didn't deserve that. All I'm
saying is that he was much more prejudiced than Victor. I
just think Victor sometimes feels guilty that he argued
against him, that's all.

BERT: Do you still love Victor?

JENNY: That's a word I prefer not to use, or even think about.

BERT: Don't you think everybody needs someone to love?

JENNY: I'm sorry – you've never talked to me like this before. I
don't really know what to say.

BERT: Would you talk to Victor?

JENNY: Bert, I've withdrawn from that war. There's no way I
want to be sucked in again. (*Pause.*) I'm sorry. I don't want
to appear uncaring. I'm not. I've just decided, after a long
and miserable period, that I have to care about me too.
(*Pause.*) I've made out a list of what you need. I'll bring
them in with me in the morning.

(*He shows no interest.*)
Would you like me to bring in the ingredients for stew?

BERT: Whatever you like.

JENNY: Bert, come on. Look, please, don't make me feel guilty about Victor. I've had enough of that.

BERT: No, no, I wasn't . . . I'm just thinking. (*Pause.*) Bring the stuff for stew. I'll tell you what – one day next week we'll take the car and do a really big shopping.

JENNY: I look forward to that.
(*She removes a list from her bag and adds to it. She closes up her bag, preparing to leave.* VICTOR *enters. He is clean-shaven, bathed, but in dressing-gown and pyjamas.*)

VICTOR: (*To* JENNY) Oh, it's you. For a minute I thought it was another one of Bert's graveyard groupies.

JENNY: I'm just ready to leave.

VICTOR: Enter Victor, exit Jenny. We're like those little figures on fancy clocks. One's for fine weather, the other for foul – so they can never appear together. (*Pause.*) Are you making any grub before you go? Or does cooking not come under your char's chores?

BERT: I'll be making a bite soon.

VICTOR: Lovely. What'll it be? Graveyard goulash? Tombstone trifle? Or what about corpse con carne?

JENNY: Victor, for goodness sake.

VICTOR: Do you know . . . Daddy . . . has a dolly?
(JENNY *looks at* BERT, *who drops his head in embarrassment.*)
She's a relative of Mother Theresa of Calcutta. Her older sister, I think.

BERT: She's just a friend, someone I met. We're just good friends.

VICTOR: See, Jenny – just met and they're already better friends than us.

JENNY: I don't want an explanation. You're perfectly entitled to have a girlfriend if you want.

VICTOR: *Girl* friend! Oh, come on, Jenny, let's get the terminology right. She's old enough to be your ma's granny.

BERT: (*Rattled*) She's younger than me. She's only 63.

VICTOR: Pensioner-snatcher, naughty boy. It's great for me – my da and his Republican moll – and my wife, the paramilitary Godfather's moll.

BERT: You're sick, do you know that? Sick.

VICTOR: Correct. Sick. Sick of her, and her cuddly killers. Sick at the very thought of you and that . . . that . . . ugly antique.

BERT: Now you listen to me . . . (*Reluctant to say anything, trying to contain his fury*) Just listen to me . . .

VICTOR: (*Checking his watch*) Five, four, three, two, one, zero. Sorry, must dash. Must get ready – my country needs me. Happy courting.
(*He goes.*)

BERT: I'll kill him. I'll kill the bastard myself. (*Slumps down.*) He's going to have to go. I don't have to take that, not in my own house, I don't.

JENNY: Don't get yourself any more worked up, come on.

BERT: (*Pause.*)
She's a widow. We met in the cemetery. Her son was murdered. His grave's just across the path from Sam's. We used to just talk in passing. 'Hello.' 'Good morning.' 'Nice day.' Nothing more than that. One day they wrecked the grave. I found her crying. They'd daubed slogans all over the headstone. They'd broken the bowl – pulled out the flowers. I just went to help her. Now he's made it sound sordid, perverted.

JENNY: No, it's not. You mustn't think like that. You mustn't allow him to make you think like that. (*Pause.*) Why did you tell him about her?

BERT: I didn't. I brought her here one night. He was supposed to be working late, and, allowing for his drinking, I expected to be in bed before he . . . (*Realizing*) I don't mean . . .

JENNY: (*Laughing*) I know you don't mean that. I wasn't thinking that.

BERT: Anyway, I would have told you . . .

JENNY: Don't worry about it. You didn't have to tell me.

BERT: I wanted to . . .

JENNY: I did wonder about all the sandwich pans – all the tuna steak and the meat pastes.

BERT: Daft, isn't it?

JENNY: Not at all.

BERT: As if he wasn't bad enough. As if he didn't have enough ammunition. I can't be as vicious as him. There's always this terrible guilt – I'll say something and something'll happen to him, before I've a chance to put it right. Like Sam.

JENNY: But, Bert, he plays on that.

BERT: I know, but he is my son. All I'm saying is that I'm afraid for him.

JENNY: I know that. I'm married to him. I lived with him. But unless he starts to worry about himself, nothing is going to change. (*Pause.*) Look, next Sunday I'll come over and make a nice big lunch – for the three of us. There's one thing about Victor – he'll never refuse a good feed.

The Donaghy house. DEIRDRE *with* THERESA.

THERESA: You need to be careful, that's all I'm saying . . .

DEIRDRE: I am careful. She's looked after them before. I just need to get away from there, and them for a while. Not that this is a great escape.

THERESA: I never left you three when you were young. Never.

DEIRDRE: Good – you can wear your campaign medals on Mother's Day. You know, the way they do on Remembrance Day.

THERESA: I would never have trusted any stranger with yous – especially a schoolgirl. The things that go on nowadays – young and foolish's right for the most of them.

DEIRDRE: Ma, she's 15, old enough. She's about fifteen stone, so she'll not have any boyfriends in. She's poor, and not at all a swinger – so she'll not be on drugs. She's vegetarian, so she'll not eat the children. Does that reassure you?

THERESA: Oh, you're the great girl for clever talk. It'll be too late when there's a tragedy. It always happens to the ones who think it'll never happen to them. (*Pause.*) Why didn't you bring them down with you?

DEIRDRE: I wanted a break – and if you don't shut up it'll not be one.

THERESA: Well, if it happens, don't say you weren't warned.

DEIRDRE: I'll put it in the paper: 'Result of an accident, comma, but my mother warned me.' (*Pause.*) Where's Joan?

THERESA: She's out the back.

DEIRDRE: All this time – she must be constipated.

THERESA: She's whitewashing the yard.

DEIRDRE: What's she doing that for?

THERESA: Because she feels it needs it. I didn't want her to bother. It gets dirty again that easy, and then once it's done you've to keep at it.

DEIRDRE: Well, that'll be no problem to Joan. She'll probably do it once a week.

THERESA: What about you? Have you had any more trouble with that one next door to you?

DEIRDRE: Trouble, she's been as nice as ninepence. She even sent me in a bowl of soup yesterday. I give it to our Kevin – in case the oul whore'd poisoned it.

THERESA: You give it to one of your kids, because you thought it might be poisoned?

DEIRDRE: I did it for their sakes. I thought, I've got three kids, but they've only got one ma.
(*She laughs at* THERESA's *shocked expression.*)
Honest, Ma, you'd believe shite was chocolate because it's brown. It was a nice drop of soup. Oh yes, I'm one of the gang now. She'll not let me pass now. It's funny really, she whistles when she talks – but she says the dentist's doing her a wee plate.

THERESA: Huh, she must have no shame. If you'd kicked two of my teeth out, I'd never have spoken to you again.

DEIRDRE: I intimidate her, you see. Keep her living in fear. If she takes any liberties, I threaten her – make faces of disapproval, or grunt. I'm a bit worried about myself. She's terrified of me and I get a great kick from seeing the fear in her face. It's a pity her man's such a wee creep or I could take him to bed as part of the spoils of war.

THERESA: Deirdre!

DEIRDRE: In future I'm only going to beat up women with good-looking, sexy husbands.
(THERESA *tut-tuts as* JOAN *comes in. There's as much whitewash on her as on the yard walls.*)

THERESA: In the name of God, you've yourself plastered.

DEIRDRE: You'd suit your hair streaked.

JOAN: It's never in my hair, is it? The wall was that rough, it kept skiting.

THERESA: Have you finished?

JOAN: Aye. I did the inside of the toilet as well.

DEIRDRE: Dead posh. Do we have to wear matching undies now?

JOAN: I saw that pigeon again.

DEIRDRE: What pigeon?

THERESA: A pigeon keeps coming round here. We think it must have been one of Peter's.

DEIRDRE: Maybe it's Peter himself – he's come back as a pigeon. That'd be great. Imagine all the people you could shite on from a great height.

THERESA: Deirdre, that's a dreadful thing to say.

DEIRDRE: It could be – reincarnation.

THERESA: That's blasphemy. What about God?

DEIRDRE: No, he's an egomaniac. He'd come back as a golden eagle.

JOAN: Or a vulture.

THERESA: In the name of all that's holy, will the pair of you shut up. That's dreadful talk. Are yous Christians at all? I don't know, sometimes you two talk like a pair of . . .

JOAN: Protestants?

The Andrews living room. BERT *is dozing in a chair.* VICTOR
enters, smoking.

VICTOR: Lunch was nice.

BERT: Uh . . . what? Oh, I must have dozed. (*Pause.*) What did
you say?

VICTOR: I said, lunch was nice.

BERT: It was a great feed, eh? I'm beginning to enjoy these
lunches. She doesn't have to cook for us, you know. It was
her own idea. It's really nice to have the three of us round the
table again, isn't it? Sitting together. That's nice, isn't it?

VICTOR: It was only lunch, not an East–West summit.

BERT: Still, we were together . . . we were talking . . . you
were talking. That's something.

VICTOR: (*A look of contempt.*) I spoke twice. I lie – three times. I
asked for the salt. I asked for the sugar. I said yes when she
asked me if I wanted more tea.

BERT: Jenny, not 'she'. She's not a she, she's your wife, Jenny.

VICTOR: My ex-wife – 'her'.

BERT: She does us proud. She's a wonderful girl.

VICTOR: You think so? I think you should take it easy. I think
you've all you can handle for the moment.

BERT: Don't cheapen everything, Victor. I'm very fond of
Jenny. Don't cheapen her.

VICTOR: Cheapen her – with what she gets from the two of us?
You've got to be joking. How much extra does she screw
you for . . . for making the lunches?

BERT: Nothing extra, she does it for nothing.

VICTOR: No wonder she eats so much – she does nothing for
nothing.

(BERT *looks at him, but decides not to pursue it any further.*
Pause.)

BERT: Theresa liked you, by the way.

VICTOR: (*Somewhat unprepared for this, so long after the event*)
Did she?

49

BERT: She's a fine woman. She's had a hard life, been through a lot.

VICTOR: Da, I'd prefer you to say Theresa thought I was an ignorant fucker – and so do you.

BERT: Ah, but she didn't, that's the point. I thought you went a bit too far, trying to be unpleasant – but she understood.

VICTOR: Did she? Are you sure she's not Mother Theresa?

BERT: You think nobody understands, but we do, son.

VICTOR: Great. Everything's all right then.

BERT: I wish I could believe that.

VICTOR: Da, for Christ's sake. (*Exasperated*) Every time you open your mouth now I hear violins. Since you met this woman you've gone soft in the bloody head. I don't see the world the way you do. I'm not in love with life the way you are. Maybe I need the love of a good woman, but I don't have it. I don't even know a good woman.

BERT: Jenny's a good woman. I'd like to see you two trying to talk.

VICTOR: Don't hold your breath.

BERT: What went wrong between you two? I've never understood that. I remember when you were going out together, you whistled, you sang, your whole life just revolved around her. When you were first married it seemed perfect. What went wrong?

VICTOR: I didn't believe even you'd be stupid enough, and wet enough, to ask a question like that. I'll tell you what went wrong. She did. When I had a few drinks, she nagged. When I had more than a few drinks, she stopped speaking to me, for days. When I felt randy, she had a headache. When I wanted to go out, she wanted to stay in. When I wanted to stay in, she wanted to go out. When I turned left, she turned right. It's no big deal, no big mystery. Some of the best marriages I know are broken ones. Things went wrong and got worse all the time. When I laughed, she cried. When I cried, she cried. When I was in, she cried. When I went out, she cried. That's about all I remember of the last six months of it . . . salty . . . tears during the day, heaving and sobbing through the night.

BERT: Why did you go with other women? You can't ask a
woman to live with that.
VICTOR: I wanted to fuck somebody who wanted to fuck me
back. I want to live in a hothouse, not a fucking freezer.
(BERT *winces*.)
Do you know what we had at the end? We had a nuclear
marriage. Neither of us had the ability to win – but we had
the means to destroy each other. And that's what we did.
BERT: So how do these things happen?
(VICTOR *shows exasperation and agitation*.)
They've happened between you and me too. We used to be
close. Until you joined the police, until all this nonsense,
these troubles started, we were friends, we had a
relationship. So what happened to that?
VICTOR: Sam, Da. Sam happened to that. From the time he got
it into his thick skull that I had stolen Jenny from him – and
you encouraged that.
BERT: That's nonsense. I'd no favourites. You were both equal
in my eyes.
VICTOR: That's not how I saw it – and it's not how I see it now.
It was bad enough when he was here, just flesh and blood,
but now . . . fuck me. The night we picked him off that
path you canonized him. I can't compete with that. I can't
compete with a saint who lives in a flower garden.
BERT: You're jealous. Jealous of a dead man, are you?
VICTOR: No, I'm not jealous of my dead brother. I'm jealous of
the person you're trying to make out he was. The way you
talk people'd think he didn't shite and piss like the rest of
us.
BERT: There's no need for that. Whatever Sam was, and
whatever I make him out to be, he's dead. Isn't that enough
for you?
VICTOR: Da, we don't talk the same language.
BERT: No, we don't. Mine doesn't have the barrack-room spice.
What strikes me as a pity is that we can't move out of
earshot of each other. We were having a conversation about
you and Jenny. About the mess you've made of your
marriage, of your whole life. Where does Sam come into it?

VICTOR: By implication, as an image. What you think he was is what you want me to be. My marriage failed because we, Jenny and me, failed. We failed each other. It wasn't all my fault. (*Pause.*) You think I'm a lousy policeman because I drink and whore. You think I get my kicks beating the heads of helpless prisoners against the walls. You've written me off in just about every area of my life – and you've been doing it for years. It's always been Sam this and Sam that. All right, I'm sorry for you. The wrong son was shot. Tough.

BERT: Now wait, hold on a minute. I've never thought that. Never. (*Distressed*) Surely you don't think . . . (*Pause.*) Victor . . .

(JENNY *comes in. Pause. Tension.*)

JENNY: I'll put the kettle on if anybody'd like more tea.

BERT: (*Still stunned by the accusation*) Jenny, he thinks I wanted him shot instead of Sam. Tell him it's not true.

VICTOR: Every time I walk through that door, and you look up, I know I'm the wrong one.

(*He goes.* JENNY *just stands.*)

BERT: It isn't true Jenny.

JENNY: No, I know – and I'm sure he doesn't really believe it either. (*Pause.*) I stayed out because I thought you two were talking. I mean really talking, not arguing.

BERT: So that's it . . .

(*She remains.* BERT *hasn't even heard her. She might not be there. Hold as the outside door slams. A car revs up and drives off at speed. Silence.*)

ACT II

SCENE 11

The hut in the cemetery. It is raining. BERT *and* THERESA *have just finished their picnic.*

THERESA: It's the first wet day we've had – here.

BERT: Yes. It's needed though.

THERESA: Yes, the flowers need it.

BERT: At least it's still warm.

THERESA: Our first wet day.

BERT: Do your daughters know about us?

THERESA: (*Taking a moment to answer*) I told Joan one day, just let it all pour out before I realized. Deirdre doesn't know. (*Pause.*) Joan hasn't really mentioned it since. (*Pause.*) We're not making much progress, are we?

BERT: Together we are – not with the families. Still, we didn't expect to really, did we?

THERESA: I don't know what we expected. We've got just to go ahead, I think. We haven't talked about what we want to do, have we?

BERT: Maybe we've been afraid to – in case we would decide it was pointless.

THERESA: Is that what we have decided?

BERT: Not me.

THERESA: Nor me. So they can just like it or lump it.

BERT: Victor never talks to me much at all now. I think that's even worse. He'll not stay in a room . . . escapes . . . runs away. If he's in a room, and I go in, or Jenny goes in, he goes out. He hasn't eat a lunch at home since our words over Sam. I just lie awake at night. I hear him tumbling in. (*Pause.*) When I hear the car stopping I hold my breath, waiting. Some night I'm going to hear the shots and it'll all be over. I know it. I'm expecting it so much, when it does happen it'll probably not register at first. (*Pause.*) It was different with Sam. For some reason I never expected it to happen to him. Yet, as soon as it happened, I was on my feet . . . at the door just as he hit the ground. It's funny, I

53

just realized, the day we had the row, Victor was right behind me, and he'd his gun in his hand. (*Pause.*) I wish I'd told him. That quick, that alert. I've never given him credit for that. Even when he bent to pick the bottles up, the gun was pointing, ready. (*Pause.*) I'd had a terrible row with Sam that morning. He'd brought a woman home. He did that, did Sam. He'd go and have a few drinks and bring a woman home. Different woman. Just ones he'd pick up. God knows where. I don't think they were prostitutes. Victor doesn't think I ever saw faults in Sam, but I did. We seemed closer because we lived together. Victor was married – he'd his own home. I always thought Sam and me were close enough – for a father and son of our ages. I used to mention the women to him, in passing – almost joking. I hoped he'd take the hint. Realize I didn't like it, stop doing it. (*Pause.*) The last one had been . . . loud, brash, very drunk . . . not a nice woman. Sam never had very good taste with women. He only ever once brought home a nice girl – Jenny. (THERESA: ???) She was Sam's girl first. She fell for Victor. Sam always resented that. He didn't love her, mind. I don't think he did. She was always set on something more serious. That's why I'm surprised the marriage failed – it was such a love match. I can't really believe it was her fault. (*Pause.*) I'm lost, Theresa. I was alienating Victor without even realizing it . . . making him feel I blamed him for everything . . . even for surviving. (*Long pause. She looks at him, but leaves the silence.*)

THERESA: You should come round. I've told Joan I'm bringing you round. My place isn't up to much, really, but it's clean. Joan never sits still, always at it. We've an outside . . . (*She realizes he's not listening. Pause.*)

I wish I was young again, Bert. Sometimes I feel even older than I am. I wonder who I'm trying to fool. Romance at my age. Then I think, well, why not? We wouldn't probably have bothered if we'd met when we were younger, would we?

BERT: Before we were married? I don't know.

THERESA: I certainly didn't mean after we were married. That's

one thing I never considered, even at the worst of times.
(*Pause.*) No, we wouldn't have bothered. Maybe we should
be grateful we've met at all. (*Pause.*) An English soldier – I
could just picture my father's face if I'd brought you home.

BERT: Was he a Republican, your father?

THERESA: Oh no, not as bad as that. He'd have had no time for
all this nonsense going on at present. He just believed we
should stay apart, English and Irish, Catholics and
Protestants.

BERT: Maybe that's fair enough. The way I was brought up,
joining the army was almost a natural process.
Discipline – that was my dad's watchword. Cold baths, long
walks, and strong laxatives. According to him all life's ills
stemmed from the bowel. So you kept it clean and clear.

THERESA: (*Laughs.*) Don't talk – we queued up for ours on a
Saturday night – didn't make Sunday much of a day of rest.
Weren't the old ones desperate?
(*Pause.*)

BERT: Yes, it would be great to be young again. Mind you, I'm
surprised I've got this far. My parents never reached their
sixties. Elsie was a young woman.

THERESA: (*Joining him*) When you think about it, though, are
we doing so badly? Being young isn't solving any problems
for those two of mine – or yours for that matter. (*Pause.*) Do
you write letters, Bert?

BERT: Letters! Who to?

THERESA: To anyone. Do you write letters?

BERT: No. I send our Madge, my sister, a Christmas card. I
scribble a note on that – just on the card. Why do you ask
that?

THERESA: Would you write me a letter?

BERT: !!!

THERESA: I'd love a love letter, even if it's just the one. It's
fascinating, when you think of people who die – and they
leave lots of letters and papers. All the papers in my life are
in one shoe box. Insurance policies, birth certificates,
marriage certificate, and death certificates – that's my life in
paper. (*Pause.*) Did you and your wife write – when you

were away in the army?

BERT: They're all destroyed years ago. Elsie wouldn't have tolerated that sort of 'clutter', as she'd have called it, about the place.

THERESA: That's sad. It would have been nice for you to have had those now, wouldn't it?

BERT: Would it? I don't know. I suppose they were pretty ordinary letters. I don't think I was much of a letter writer.

THERESA: What about her letters to you?

BERT: I didn't keep those. There was no point. She never wrote very exciting letters as I remember it. Lots of advice – about dry socks, well aired, warm vests. Warnings about the dangers of bad women – especially foreigners who gave themselves to soldiers. I'd almost to sign a declaration before I was allowed back into bed with her when I came home. She was a funny woman.

THERESA: (*Quietly emotional*) I feel quite sad, Bert. We've led such dull, boring lives, haven't we? No wonder they find the idea of a love affair between us funny. Look at us . . .

BERT: (*Gently putting an arm around her shoulders*) Hey, don't get upset about it. All right, we haven't set the world alight. They'll not have to sit up late at night sorting out what we leave behind. But so what? We're just ordinary people. We're not pretending to be anything more than that, are we? Let them laugh. Why should we care? In the end they'll have to realize, and just judge us as ordinary people. I'll write you a letter – a love letter.

The Donaghy house. JOAN *is sitting.* THERESA *is applying make-up, preparing to go out with* BERT. *She isn't very skilful at making up. She keeps applying too much, and then rubbing it off.* JOAN *smirks at her efforts.*

THERESA: I wish you'd stop sitting there sniggering, and give me a hand.

JOAN: I'd bring you in the trowel, if I knew where it was.

THERESA: Those ones in Boots are great at telling you what will suit madam, and what won't suit madam. They don't tell you it takes years to learn how to put it on properly. (*Inspecting herself in the mirror and then turning to face* JOAN) Have I still got too much on?

JOAN: (*Inspecting her carefully*) Well, that depends . . . (*Stops deliberately.*)

THERESA: On what?

JOAN: On whether you're really going to the pictures, or to a fancy-dress ball, as a clown.

THERESA: Well, will you do more than just sit and snigger at me. Give me a hand.
(JOAN *rises slowly.*)
Jesus, Mary and Joseph, you'd try the patience of a saint. God forgive me.

JOAN: Do you think he will?

THERESA: (*Irritated*) Do I think who'll what?

JOAN: Do you think God'll forgive you?
(*She starts rubbing away some of* THERESA's *lipstick.*)

THERESA: (*Pulling away*) For goodness sake, don't smudge my lipstick.

JOAN: I'm not smudging it, I'm reclaiming part of your face. (*Rubbing*) You don't want him to think you've got a bigger mouth than you have.

THERESA: You just be careful, or I'll give you a thick ear.

JOAN: Save your aggression, it could come in useful later on.
(THERESA *just gives her a dirty look.*)

57

Will I be a bridesmaid?

THERESA: Will you give it over.

JOAN: You always used to talk about Elizabeth Taylor because she got remarried.

THERESA: Remarried? That hussy was married half-a-dozen times.

JOAN: Yes, but she had to have number two before she could have number three, didn't she?

THERESA: I'm not getting married. I'm only going to the pictures.

JOAN: Has he asked you yet?

THERESA: Are you right in the head? We're friends, that's all.

JOAN: That's just what she said about Richard Burton.

THERESA: You know, I think you're worse than that other one. Would you rather I just sat in the corner and waited to die?

JOAN: People are going to talk.

THERESA: Let them talk. When they're talking about us they're leaving somebody else alone.

JOAN: Oh aye. I could just hear you if it was one of us.

THERESA: Sure I'm always on at you to go out with boys.

JOAN: Boys – there's a quare difference between me going out with 'a boy' and you going out with a grandad.

THERESA: Wouldn't I look pretty sick going out with a boy? (*The bantering takes on a greater edge now*.)

JOAN: You'll look pretty sick anyway. (*Pause*.)

THERESA: (*Emotional*) Honest to God, why do I have to take all this abuse? Why? I'm having a perfectly respectable relationship with a man my own age, that's all.

JOAN: I thought you said he was 68?

THERESA: (*Giving her a fierce look*) Is it a crime? Am I not allowed to be happy? I've been alone for a long time now – so who am I hurting?

JOAN: People don't usually have love affairs at your age.

THERESA: No, they're rarely fortunate enough. I've met a nice man, a good man. We're both widowed. We've both lost a son. We've our suffering in common. It brought us together. (*Pause*.) Now we've fallen in love, that's all.

58

JOAN: (*Gazing at her*) In love? You're in love?

THERESA: (*Exasperated*) Of course I'm in love. Do you think I'd cake my face with this shit, God forgive me, if I wasn't in love?

JOAN: (*Stunned*) I hope you don't say this outside.

THERESA: Of course I do. I tell everybody I meet. I stop people and say, 'Do you know I'm in love, and I'm 63?' I'm going to have it tattooed on my breasts. 'I am' on the right one, 'in love' on the left one.

JOAN: It isn't funny. (*Pause.*) It's not. It's no joking matter. So you're in love. What are you going to do – marry him?

THERESA: If he asks me, I might.

JOAN: Church or chapel? Who'll change?

THERESA: We're too old to bother with that. Nobody needs to change.

JOAN: I don't want a stepfather, especially not a Protestant one. Where will you live? Here? Or with him and his policeman son? Maybe you could build yourselves a reinforced concrete bunker.

THERESA: You can say what you like.

JOAN: Wait till Deirdre hears about this.

THERESA: I don't care about Deirdre. This is my last chance of . . . of . . . (*Pause.*) He's given me a bit of happiness – for the first time in years.

JOAN: You were supposed to be tending your son's grave – not hunting for eligible widowers.

THERESA: I was attending my son's grave. Maybe you and that other one would be happier if I got down into it with him.

JOAN: It was an insult to him.

THERESA: Who are you to criticize? You and your sister never bothered. Bert was the only one I had when it was vandalized.

JOAN: Huh, vandalized. He probably did it himself, just for an excuse to chat you up. I suppose he'd been making eyes at you for weeks. I think it's disgusting. I think it's the most disgusting, obscene thing I've ever heard of. Look at you . . . you're old . . . look . . . made up like something out of a circus.

(THERESA *just looks at her, hurt. Long pause.*)

You're a different religion – and you pick your son's grave as a courting place.

THERESA: His son's buried there too . . .

JOAN: I couldn't care less about his son. His son wasn't my brother. His son wasn't murdered just because he was a Catholic.

THERESA: Well, he isn't a Catholic – but there are innocent Protestants.

JOAN: I'd love to meet one.

THERESA: (*Looking at her for a moment, deciding*) Aye, well, you will. I'll bring Bert round.

JOAN: What for?

THERESA: Because this is my house and I want him here.

JOAN: What about me?

THERESA: You tell me what about you. Obviously he'd like to meet you.

JOAN: Why does he want to meet me?

THERESA: (*Looking at her*) I can't imagine. (*Doing some more to her make-up*) What's that like now?

JOAN: (*Down*) It's fine.

THERESA: Seriously, don't just say that to get rid of me. It's not too heavy?

JOAN: It's fine, I've said. (*Pause.*) What's the picture?

THERESA: I don't know. I'll let him decide. Sure I don't like the pictures anyway.

JOAN: So why are you going?

THERESA: Where else is there? I'm not interested in sitting in pubs. I'm too old for dancing. You're not making it easy to bring him back here.

JOAN: Bring him back here if you like. (*Pause.*) I'm sorry for saying those things. I didn't mean them.

THERESA: They wouldn't have hurt if they'd been rumours. I think we are being silly. I'll feel a fool in the queue . . . all the young ones.

JOAN: You'll hardly be competing with them for the back row.

THERESA: You do think it's disgusting, don't you?

JOAN: Mum . . .

THERESA: No, the truth, tell me the truth.

JOAN: It's your own business.

THERESA: (*Taking a long look at her*) I see.
(*She sits down. They both sit in silence for a moment.*)

JOAN: What time are you seeing him at?
(THERESA *doesn't answer. She is fighting back tears.*)
Mum . . . Mum. . . ?
(THERESA *rises slowly.*)

THERESA: I'm going up to lie down.

JOAN: (*As she goes*) Mum, don't do this to me. (*Screaming*)
Mum.
(THERESA *stops and looks at her.*)
(*Emotional*) All right, go to bed . . . go on . . . go. Let your
'nice' man stand about in the cold. Let him realize how
much he really means to you.
(JOAN *is working herself up into a state of hysteria. It is clearly
evident now why she is on valium.*)

THERESA: Joan, pull yourself together.

JOAN: Go you on up and lie down. Don't worry about me. I'm
not an old man standing in the cold, wondering what I've
done wrong. I don't care. Go on, go on . . .
(THERESA *goes and embraces* JOAN *and tries to calm her down.*
JOAN *starts to cry.*)

THERESA: Oh, come on, Joan . . . come on, love . . . don't get
yourself all worked up. It's all right . . . it's all right . . .
please. I'll go out in a minute.
(*She continues to hold* JOAN, *as she begins to calm down.*)

SCENE 13

The cemetery. BERT *is sitting, sipping tea. His unopened packet of sandwiches sits beside him.* JOAN *approaches . . . hesitates . . . comes forward.*

JOAN: Excuse me, I wondered . . . are you Bert?

BERT: (*Surprised, a little wary*) Yes.

JOAN: I'm Joan Donaghy, Theresa's daughter.

BERT: (*Rising hurriedly*) Is your mother all right?

JOAN: Yes, she's fine.

BERT: (*Offering his hand*) How do you do? Won't you sit down? Would you like some tea?

JOAN: No, thank you.

(*She sits. Pause. Awkwardness.*)

My mother got your letter this morning. I didn't read it of course. (*Pause.*) I saw you here yesterday.

BERT: Yes. I thought I saw someone at the grave. Then I thought it must be the one next to it. I've never seen anyone but your mother at it.

JOAN: I've never been to it before. It took me ages to find it. I never wanted to see it. I wish I hadn't. I just wanted to imagine it. I wish he'd been buried in a quiet country churchyard. I'd like it to be under a tree, in a corner, with flowers . . . flowers growing naturally. (*Pause.*) My mother doesn't know I'm here.

BERT: She didn't want to come herself?

JOAN: She did, but . . . the reason she didn't turn up at the cinema the other night was because of me . . . (*Pause. Looking at him*) I wasn't well.

BERT: She told me . . . (*Awkward*) about your nerves.

JOAN: (*Looking into his face*) We had a row. It was about you.

BERT: A row about me?

JOAN: It was my fault. I just started on her. She got upset. I said some silly, hurtful things. Then I got very upset because she decided not to go out. It's like that you see. I get upset, then I sort of get upset at getting upset . . . and

it gets worse . . . if you see what I mean.
(*Pause.*)

BERT: You don't approve of us then?

JOAN: I don't know. It's just a surprise. I mean . . .

BERT: I know. We're old, we should know better. It surprised us too, you know. I mean it just happened.

JOAN: It's not for me to say.

BERT: Is it because I'm a Protestant?

JOAN: There's that as well.

BERT: You were very close to your brother, your mother says.

JOAN: I feel very bitter about the people who killed my brother.

BERT: I feel very bitter about the people who killed my son, but I know it wasn't you, or your mother – so I can't be bitter at you.

JOAN: Well, I just feel bitter against all Protestants. Another thing, what are people going to say?

BERT: Does it matter what people say?

JOAN: It matters if they blow my mother's kneecaps off – or attack our house. You used to be a soldier and all.

BERT: That was years and years ago. Long before the troubles ever started.

JOAN: The troubles didn't start in sixty-nine. They just continued. They've been going on for hundreds of years. Round our way they'd probably think you were a spy.

BERT: A spy? (*Laughs.*) At my age?

JOAN: I don't think age has got anything to do with it. (*Pause.*) Why can't you and my mother just be friends here? Lots of old people are just friends in graveyards, or parks. They don't want to get married, or live together. They don't want to go to each other's houses and drag their whole families into it. It's just silly. I don't mean to be ignorant, but you're not just old – you're very old. You're nearly 70.

BERT: I'm 68.

JOAN: Well that's nearly 70.

BERT: It might be nearly 70 but I'm still only 68.

JOAN: I'm sorry, I'm being very cheeky.

BERT: My son was a lot more cheeky with your mother. (*Pause.*) You're younger than I expected, and prettier.

JOAN: I look younger than I am.

BERT: What did you do?

JOAN: I was a nurse – a career girl. I was on duty the night our Peter was shot.

BERT: Good grief, do you mean. . . ?

JOAN: No, I just heard someone had been brought in, and that he'd died. The only thing on my mind was the phone call I was expecting from my boyfriend. I was on night duty. Our Peter had rang me. He asked me if I could come and give him a lift home during my break. (*Pause. Emotional*) I said no, I was waiting for a phone call.
(*They sit in silence.*)

BERT: I had a row with my son, on the morning of the day he was murdered. I'm sure though he didn't think that meant I'd stopped loving him.

JOAN: My mother doesn't know about that. How do you think she'd feel if she knew that? He'd be alive today but for me. Your son was different. They wanted to kill him, he was picked out. My brother just happened to be in the wrong place at the wrong time – and all because his sister was too selfish to give him a lift. (*Fights hard to control her tears.*) Will you tell her?

BERT: Tell her? Of course I won't tell her. Why would I tell her? It wasn't really your fault. I mean, you weren't to know.

JOAN: We're not talking about something simple. We're talking about life and death. My decision was the difference between life and death for my brother. (*Long pause.*) Do you know something?

BERT: ???

JOAN: (*Quietly*) The boy I was expecting the phone call from was a Protestant. Before he came into my life I'd have done anything for our Peter. I don't know why I told you that.

BERT: My son thinks I wanted him to die in his brother's place. He thinks his dead brother was my favourite. He thinks he's still my favourite. I'm really glad you've told me – you've helped me to make a decision. I'm going to talk to him. I like you, Joan.

64

JOAN: (*Smiling*) Like me – you know nothing about me. It's easy when you've no one to jump at the first likely person you see. Can you and my mother really be in love after such a short time?

BERT: We've probably only got a short time – that helps the process. I do like you though – even if you do disapprove of me.

JOAN: I'd like you to come home with me.

(*Pause. He looks alarmed.*)

Don't look so frightened. If I tell my mother what I've done, she'll never be able to face you again. But if you just turn up with me it'll be all right – and she does want to see you.

BERT: I don't know.

(*She smiles at him and he smiles in return – but he's still uncertain.*)

JOAN: (*Rising*) Come on, Bert. You're the eldest, it's up to you to make the gesture.

(*He hesitates a moment, then starts to pack up his stuff.*)

The Donaghy house. THERESA *is sitting. She takes out Bert's letter. It is written on both sides of a single sheet. She has read it before and does so again.* DEIRDRE *bounces in.* THERESA *hastily pushes the letter into her pocket, looks flustered.* DEIRDRE *is in a highly nervous state and keeps pacing the room during the scene.*

DEIRDRE: Have you got the final notice for the electric or something?

THERESA: No, no, it's nothing. (*Pause.*) How are you?

DEIRDRE: I feel all right, but I must look terrible because I seem to have frightened the shite out of you. Maybe I should have knocked and waited for you to open the door. (*Pause.*) So who was the letter from?

THERESA: (*Slightly annoyed*) Nobody, nobody. (*Pause.*) Will you sit down and stop hopping about like that.

DEIRDRE: I don't want to sit down. Where's Joan?

THERESA: Out. (*Pause.*) She's gone for a walk.

DEIRDRE: A walk – according to you the other day I thought she was cracking up again.

THERESA: Will you for goodness sake sit down.

DEIRDRE: I don't want to sit down. They're my feet I'm walking on.

THERESA: It's very irritating that – pacing up and down. It irritates my eyes, because I can't ignore it.

DEIRDRE: I'm leaving, Ma. I'm getting out.

THERESA: (*Looking at her*) Getting out where to?

DEIRDRE: England.

THERESA: What are you talking about? You've got three wee children.

DEIRDRE: I'm taking them with me.

THERESA: (*Concerned*) Deirdre, love . . . (*Angry*) For crying out loud, will you sit down.
(*Pause.* DEIRDRE *does so.*)
What are you going to do in England, with three wee children?

DEIRDRE: I'm going, that's all. I have to get away. I can't take any more.

THERESA: Look, love, I know it isn't easy for you here, but . . . well, you've got friends here. You've got me and Joan here. Over there you'll have nobody. Where will you live? What'll you do for money? You can't just go over there nowadays and live on the National Assistance.

DEIRDRE: We'll get something. They'll not let us starve.

THERESA: No, they'll probably send you straight back – especially when they find out about him.

DEIRDRE: I'll use a false name. I'll think of something. I've got to get away, I've got to. Do you have any money? You've something in the post office . . . I'll pay you back . . . just to get me settled.

THERESA: Deirdre, for goodness sake, be practical. How could you get a job? Who would look after the kids when you were at work?

DEIRDRE: I could always pay a babysitter.

THERESA: You couldn't afford to live over there, pay rent, feed and clothe you all, and pay a full-time babysitter.

DEIRDRE: I screamed this morning. I screamed and threw three cups against the wall.

THERESA: Where were the children?

DEIRDRE: Ducking. (*Pause.*) It happens all the time up there – women screaming, for all sorts of reasons. That's what we mean by the dawn chorus.

(THERESA *looks at her for a moment.*)

THERESA: You're not running off with another man, are you?

DEIRDRE: Oh aye, isn't the country just full of men dying to look after another man's three kids. If I could get a man life might be bearable.

THERESA: Why don't you try for a wee part-time job here? You could do home help or something.

DEIRDRE: Ma, I want away from here.

THERESA: Well, I just don't see how you're going to manage.

DEIRDRE: You could help me.

THERESA: Deirdre, I don't think the little money I have in the post office would help you very much at all.

DEIRDRE: (*Looking at her*) There is something else you could do for me.

(*They look at each other for a moment.* THERESA *begins to realize what is on* DEIRDRE'*s mind.*)

THERESA: No, no. Deirdre, I am not, at my age, going to take on three young children.

DEIRDRE: Ma, all I want is a chance. You know you'll not be left with them. I love them, you know that. They're not strangers – they're your grandchildren.

THERESA: Yes, and I can cope with them as that – not as children I have to look after all day, every day. I'm not able for it. Goodness, the odd times I do look after them they have me exhausted.

DEIRDRE: I'll send you money home every week, I promise.

THERESA: I'm not fit for it.

(*Pause.*)

DEIRDRE: You don't realize how serious this is. You don't know how badly I need to get away. I'm going mad. I'm just screaming inside. I'm sometimes afraid I'm going to do something to me, or one of the kids.

THERESA: You'll have to tell Joe. You can't just walk out on him, without any warning.

DEIRDRE: Do you know what would happen if I told him? He'd set his mates on me. I wouldn't be allowed to go anywhere. Why should I have to suffer for what he did?

THERESA: You shouldn't – but there's even less reason why I should.

DEIRDRE: You hate my children.

THERESA: Don't talk absolute rubbish.

DEIRDRE: I know lots of grandparents who've brought up their grandchildren.

THERESA: At my age? Ach, Deirdre, love, I'm not being nasty, or selfish – I just couldn't cope with it. Suppose there's an amnesty?

DEIRDRE: I'll cut my throat. (*Pause.*) Do you think what Joe did was wrong?

THERESA: Of course I think it was wrong. I think the people who murdered our Peter were wrong. He was innocent. At least the ones Joe shot were involved.

DEIRDRE: (*Looking at her*) They were like our Peter, Ma. They were somebody's sons . . . somebody's brothers . . . one of them was somebody's husband and the father of three children. (*Pause.*) How will I bring up my children, Ma? What will I tell them? Your Uncle Peter was killed by murderers – but your da's a hero for murdering others?

THERESA: They'll have to make up their own minds when they're old enough.

DEIRDRE: Ma, we live in Northern Ireland. My children won't have their own minds when they're old enough.

(*Pause. They glance at each other. Silence.*)

I've never asked you for anything, never. Please, Ma, will you help me now?

The Andrews house. A box and two suitcases sit. Pause. JENNY
*enters, her coat on, just arrived. As she is removing her coat and taking
in the cases and the box,* VICTOR *comes in, carrying another case.*

VICTOR: I thought I'd missed you.

JENNY: I'm late today. I'd something to do in town. Are you
leaving?

VICTOR: No, they're a new line in lunchboxes and I'm going for a
picnic.

JENNY: Have you and your father had another row?

VICTOR: I don't know, I haven't spoken to him lately.

JENNY: Doesn't he know you're going?

VICTOR: You can tell him, save me writing a note.

JENNY: You mean you're just going to walk out – without even
saying a word to him?

VICTOR: Tell him I said goodbye.

JENNY: Victor, why are you doing this to him?

VICTOR: I'm a cruel bastard.

JENNY: You're certainly trying hard enough.

VICTOR: You'd be surprised how little effort it takes.

JENNY: Where are you going?

VICTOR: I thought I might move in with you for a couple of
weeks.

JENNY: I'm going to get started.

VICTOR: (*As she leaves*) Jenny . . . I would.

JENNY: No, thanks.

VICTOR: Why won't you give me another chance?

JENNY: I've given you all the chances any man ever needed.

VICTOR: It would be different this time. I've been out, away from
you . . . I'm more aware of what I've missed . . . of what I
had and messed up.

JENNY: I didn't think you were missing much.

VICTOR: Listen to me . . .

JENNY: Victor, I've heard it all before.

VICTOR: A trial . . . a month . . . if it doesn't work I'll move

70

straight out again. I'll stop drinking. I'll stay at home every
night . . .

JENNY: Except when you're on duty.

VICTOR: Wouldn't you like to eat?

JENNY: I'd like to eat – and sleep, and like to relax, and I'd like
to be reasonably happy. You didn't even know you'd see
me today. You thought I'd been and gone. Why do you
cheapen everything?

VICTOR: The fact that I took advantage of bumping into you
doesn't make me any less keen to come back. When I left, I
didn't take any decision never to come back.

JENNY: The decision wasn't yours – and it isn't yours now.

VICTOR: Why did you start making the lunches here? What was
that all about?

JENNY: It was about trying to get us all sitting down together,
eating together in a civilized, friendly way.
(*He just stands looking at her, saying nothing. She stands,
uncertain.*)

VICTOR: Well, this isn't getting us anywhere.

JENNY: Can I know where you're going?

VICTOR: Why? Do you want to know which areas of town to
avoid?

JENNY: Is there any need to be unfriendly, just because we can't
live together? Can't we just accept that we lead different
lives . . . live in different worlds, and just be friendly with
each other?

VICTOR: What about sex? I mean, couldn't we have the odd,
civil, friendly screw?

JENNY: You never needed me for that.
(*He stands, smirking, lighting a cigarette.*)
What's so funny?
(*He shrugs.*)
Are you going to live with someone, Victor? Are you going
to live with another woman?

VICTOR: Are you jealous?

JENNY: (*Looking at him*) I see. God, but you are a child, and not
a very bright one at that. No, I'm not jealous. You run
along Victor. I hope it's what you want.

71

VICTOR: It's what I need, someone to come home to. I'm lonely, you see. I hate coming back to this place . . . hate the emptiness . . . hate the silence.

JENNY: The silence was of your making.

VICTOR: No, it wasn't, not really. I just stopped speaking, but that was just reluctant recognition of the fact that we had no language.

JENNY: What did you expect, the way you carried on?

VICTOR: That's not what I mean, Jenny. You and my da have a language – it doesn't matter whether you actually speak or not. If you want to talk to each other, you have the means to do so. We hadn't that. Me and my da hadn't that.

JENNY: Does the one you're moving in with have it?

VICTOR: She doesn't need to have, yet.

JENNY: Where will you go if you discover she hasn't?

VICTOR: Who knows? It's not a pressing worry. I can keep up an act long enough to find an exit.

JENNY: What sort of a life's that?

VICTOR: Unsatisfactory – but on-going. It's where I'm at, as the saying goes.

JENNY: Who is she? Is she a policewoman?

VICTOR: Does it matter?

JENNY: No. Is she married? (*He laughs.*) Does she have kids?

VICTOR: You are jealous, aren't you?

JENNY: To tell you the truth, I don't know. I shouldn't really be surprised, but I am. I've been washing more socks and shirts recently . . .

VICTOR: I don't have to go – I'm serious now – if you were prepared to give it a go.

JENNY: I couldn't trust my own motives at the moment.

VICTOR: At least you'll not be able to say you weren't given a choice. No, I don't really want back with you Jenny, I think I've found what I want, for the moment at least. (*He picks up two of the cases and makes for the door.*)

JENNY: I didn't tell you what I was doing in town. (*He stops and looks at her.*) I was seeing a solicitor. I'm filing for a divorce. (*He stands gazing at her. Pause.*)

The Donaghy house. DEIRDRE *is standing, ready to go.*

DEIRDRE: Well, I'm going. (*Glances out of the window.*) Who does our Joan know who drives a red Mini?

THERESA: Our Joan. . . ?

DEIRDRE: Our Joan. Don't tell me she's got herself a sugar daddy. She's with some oul fella in a red Mini.

THERESA: (*Jumping to her feet, dropping the letter and going to look out*) Jesus, Mary and Joseph, it is. I'm sure those kids think you're lost. Hadn't you better run on?

DEIRDRE: They're all right. This I want to see. I've heard of girls wanting a father figure, but never a great-grandfather figure.

(THERESA *is frantic, pulls at herself, runs her hands through her hair, panic-stricken.*)

You've dropped your letter. (*Pointing*) There.

THERESA: (*Frantically grabbing up the letter, crumpling it*) Will you come away from the window. They'll think you're staring at them.

DEIRDRE: Aye, well, I am.

(JOAN *enters, ushering* BERT *in. For a moment nobody speaks.*)

JOAN: Deirdre, this is Bert.

DEIRDRE: (*Shaking hands, amused*) I'm pleased to meet you, Bert. (*To* JOAN) Crafty, you kept this quiet.

JOAN: (*Puzzled, glancing at a speechless* THERESA) You what?

THERESA: (*Offering her hand to a surprised* BERT) Is it Bert, did you say? I'm pleased to meet you. Deirdre's Joan's sister. She's just going. Her children are expecting her. Sit down, won't you.

(*He does.*)

DEIRDRE: There's no great rush. I'm always keen to welcome strangers into the family, make them feel at home. Sit you down too, Joan. Ma . . . mmm . . . I'm sure Joan's friend could use a cup of tea. You'll have to excuse her, Bert, (*with a look to* THERESA) I don't think she's ever seen a man before.

(JOAN, BERT *and* THERESA *sit transfixed. Nobody is sure who should speak next – and even less sure about what should be said.*)

(*Looking at each in turn*) I take it you and my mum have never met before, Bert?

(*He looks from* DEIRDRE *to* THERESA, *stunned, shakes his head vaguely.*)

She's not feeling herself today. It must have been the letter. (*To* BERT) She received a letter this morning – but she's destroyed it now.

THERESA: (*Almost shouting, as she pulls out the letter*) No, I haven't. (*Quieter, as she tries to straighten out the crumpled letter*) It just got a bit creased, that's all.

BERT: (*Half-rising*) If I've called at a bad time . . .

DEIRDRE: (*Insistent, signalling him to sit*) Not at all. (*With a look at her mother*) She had a stroke recently and it's paralysed the side of her brain that deals with good manners. (*Sharply, making* THERESA *jump*) Mother, would you for goodness sake make the poor man a cup of tea.

BERT: (*Louder than he intended, as* THERESA *rises*) No. (*Quieter*) I mean, it's all right. I don't want tea, thank you. I'd a flaskful up in the cemetery.

DEIRDRE: (*Her turn to be puzzled*) The cemetery – are you a gravedigger?

BERT: I'm late . . . ah . . .

DEIRDRE: There's no great rush, sure you're only in. How long have you been a gravedigger?

BERT: I'm not a gravedigger. (*Rising*) Could I use your toilet?

THERESA: The toilet. . . ?

JOAN: It's out the back, outside. (*He goes, mumbling his thanks.*)

DEIRDRE: Joan, I hate to say it, but if he's not a gravedigger, I think you've picked up a bloody corpse.

THERESA: Deirdre, you'd better go.

DEIRDRE: Ma, will you shut up about me going. The kids are fine. Jasus, if you're that worried about them you'd have done the wee favour I asked you.

THERESA: All right, I will. If you go now, I will.

(DEIRDRE *looks from one to the other.* JOAN *drops her head.*)

DEIRDRE: What the hell is going on here? Joan, how long has this been going on?

JOAN: ???

DEIRDRE: How long have you being going with him?

JOAN: I'm not . . .

THERESA: (*Cutting in, as* BERT *reappears*) He goes with me. (*Silence.*)

DEIRDRE: I can see now why you didn't want my kids about the place. It wouldn't do for youngsters to see their granny necking. Do you have children, Mr. . . ?

BERT: Andrews, Bert Andrews. Yes, I've a son.

THERESA: Bert had another son, but he was murdered, the same as our Peter. That's how we met . . . in the cemetery . . . at the graves. We just met . . . started talking . . . things just happened . . . and we're very fond of each other.

DEIRDRE: Why was your son murdered?

BERT: (*With a glance to* THERESA) He was a part-time UDR man.

DEIRDRE: Well, then, it wasn't the same as our Peter. Our Peter was a full-time innocent Catholic. (*Pause.*) What does your other son do, Mr Andrews?

THERESA: Deirdre, there's no call for this.

DEIRDRE: I'm curious to learn about my mother's 'man'. After all, if you two are silly enough to get involved at your ages, you're probably silly enough for anything.

THERESA: This is my house and I've said that's enough.

BERT: (*Stung, firmly*) My other son is a policeman.

DEIRDRE: Lovely – just the mixture we need in this family. I take it my 'ma' has told you all about us?

BERT: I know some things . . .

THERESA: Bert, I'd rather you went on now. Please.

BERT: I can look after myself, Theresa. I've nothing to be ashamed of . . . (*To* DEIRDRE) And I'm certainly not ashamed of my sons.

DEIRDRE: I take it, then, she's told you about Joe, my husband.

THERESA: Deirdre, I want you to go. Go and leave us alone.

DEIRDRE: Leave you alone, yes. Go back and rot up in that

bloody estate, because you're too busy with your 'friend' to look after my children.

THERESA: That's between us. It's got nothing to do with Bert.

DEIRDRE: Hasn't it?

JOAN: Please stop it, Deirdre.

DEIRDRE: You shut up. We all know about your bloody nerves. It didn't stop your going to the boneyard to bring . . . Bert . . . home. Christ, I've heard of going messages for your ma, but this is ridiculous.

BERT: I'm going. I'm sorry you should feel so hostile, Deirdre . . .

DEIRDRE: Ah, but, Bert, you don't know why I'm so hostile. You don't know this family's guilty little secret.

BERT: I'm sure whatever it is it's got nothing to do with me.

DEIRDRE: Oh, but it has. Believe me, it has.

THERESA: Stop it, will you. I'm not seeing Bert. We've stopped, it's over. (*Pause. She looks at him.*) You don't need to reveal any secrets. There's nothing you need to break up.

JOAN: I'm sorry about this, Bert, I really am.

THERESA: I'll leave you out to your car.

BERT: (*Shaking hands with* JOAN) Goodbye, Joan. I'm glad at least that I got the opportunity to meet you.
(*He offers his hand to* DEIRDRE.)

DEIRDRE: You're English, aren't you?

BERT: Yes – and an ex-soldier, in case you're running out of reasons to hate me.

DEIRDRE: You've really got it all going for you. It's funny how things can change. When we were young we weren't allowed to go out with Protestants – let alone ex-soldiers whose family made up half the bloody security forces.

BERT: You get wiser as you get older. It might even happen to you. The really funny thing is that you're so like my son it isn't true.

DEIRDRE: You should have brought him with you. The one I've got is . . .

THERESA: (*Screaming at her*) I've told you there's no need for that now.

DEIRDRE: Well, if there's no need, then it doesn't matter one way or the other, does it?

THERESA: You vicious wee bastard . . . (*Breaking down*) God forgive me.

BERT: Look, why don't we just say goodbye? That's all we need to say.

(*He offers his hand again.*)

DEIRDRE: You really are a bloody Englishman, aren't you? Before you leave this house I want you to know something. My husband is an IRA man. He's serving a life sentence for murdering members of the security forces.

(*There is a long pause.* BERT *gazes at her. She returns his stare. Then he turns it on* THERESA. JOAN *tentatively puts out a hand and touches his arm. He turns and leaves. Silence.*)

THERESA: Why did you do that, Deirdre?

DEIRDRE: You're old. Why should you have what I can't have? You're old . . . you've had your life . . .

(*She looks at* THERESA. *Pause.* THERESA *offers her arms and* DEIRDRE *collapses into them.*)

The Andrews living room. BERT *is there with* JENNY.

JENNY: Do you think she should have told you?

BERT: Of course she should. It's not a very nice way to find out
a thing like that.

JENNY: She probably just needed more time . . . more time to
learn to trust you. After all she's not responsible for her
son-in-law.

BERT: It's not that . . . it's not just that . . . it's the sort of
family they must be.

JENNY: Come on, Bert, maybe he wasn't like that when they
got married. Why don't you go and see her again – talk
it out?

BERT: I don't think it would really make any difference. It's as
if it was a spell and it's been broken now. (*Pause.*) Surely
it's up to her to make the first move?

JENNY: Is it? She probably thinks you'll not want to know her
now. You should write to her – arrange to meet somewhere,
away from the house.

BERT: I did that before. She ignored it. The daughter came of
her own free will. She seemed a nice girl. She's really
putting herself through it.

JENNY: Anybody would in those circumstances.

BERT: Yes, but I mean we all do things that we wouldn't do, if
we could foresee the circumstances later.

JENNY: You should think of that now, with you and Theresa.
You're too old to let it lie, Bert.

BERT: Suppose I do go up and she says she meant it?

JENNY: Then you'll know. You'll also know that you left the
door open, so you'll not run about endlessly wondering.
(*Pause.*) You're probably thinking I'm a right one to be
giving anyone advice on these matters.

BERT: Knowing for sure . . . you're right.

JENNY: I could do you a flask and some sandwiches . . . If she's
anxious, that's probably where she'll make for.

BERT: Going and her not being there's more frustrating than not going at all.

JENNY: I'll go for you if you like.

BERT: ???

JENNY: I'll go to her house, talk to her . . . if that would make it easier?

BERT: No, maybe she's just being more realistic than me. (*Rising*) No, the whole thing was daft from the outset. (*Pause.*) Have you thought any more about what I said – about you moving in here?

JENNY: Yes, but I've reached no conclusion yet. I'm still thinking.

BERT: I'd like to have you around.

JENNY: How do you think Victor would react?

BERT: I couldn't give a damn about Victor. (*Pause.*) I'm going out for a mouthful of air.

The Andrews house. The early hours of the morning. BERT *enters, in pyjamas and dressing-gown, followed by a slightly drunk* VICTOR.

BERT: Do you want to wake the whole place, banging like that? What the hell do you want at this time of the morning? It's three o'clock.

VICTOR: Ten to three. Two fifty. Is Jenny here?

BERT: The place is cleaner since you left. We don't need a night shift.

VICTOR: You really put the boot in, didn't you, Da?

BERT: ???

VICTOR: Ah, come on, not the innocent citizen look, spare me that. You put her up to it, didn't you?

BERT: I put nobody up to nothing. You're drunk.

VICTOR: Tipsy, not drunk. Steady of hand (*Taking out his gun and holding it at arm's length*) and mind.

BERT: Put that gun away. Half of you cowboys shouldn't be trusted with weapons. (*Pushing* VICTOR's *extended arm down*) Put it away.

VICTOR: Bitch. I'll shove it up her arse and pull the bloody trigger. Who does she think she is? Nobody divorces me and gets away with it.

BERT: How many have tried?

VICTOR: What . . . what do you mean?

BERT: Never mind. Put that gun in your pocket and away up to bed.

VICTOR: I've got a bed somewhere else now – with something warm and soft in it.

BERT: You shouldn't be driving in that state.

VICTOR: I've driven drunker than this. This is nothing. This is only tipsy. You've never seen me really drunk.

BERT: No, not half I haven't. Look, Victor, I'm tired, I was asleep. Let's talk things over in the morning.

VICTOR: Did you tell her to divorce me?

BERT: I told her nothing.

VICTOR: Liar. I can see you at it – typical bloody English, Da . . . all on the line, proper and correct . . . legal, sealed and signed.

BERT: I had nothing to do with it. Now I'm going to bed.

VICTOR: (*Raising the gun and pointing it at* BERT) You're going fucking nowhere. She never thought of a divorce. You talked her into it. Now you'd better talk her out of it – otherwise I'll blow your bloody head off.

BERT: (*Going until the gun's touching his chest*) You put that gun away now. Otherwise, so help me, I'll take it off you and give you the thrashing of your life.

VICTOR: You? You thrash me? Don't make me laugh. (*Pause. Puts the gun in his pocket. Takes his coat off.*) Who are you going to thrash, old man?

BERT: Go to bed, Victor.

(BERT *just stands and stares him out.*)

VICTOR: (*Slumping into a chair*) I don't want her to divorce me, Da.

BERT: You don't have a very strong argument, if you're conducting it from another woman's bed.

VICTOR: I still love Jenny. I just don't know how to tell her.

BERT: Staying sober, getting yourself in hand might help.

VICTOR: She wouldn't give me the chance.

BERT: You want to start with the chance. She wants to know you're worth a chance, before she risks it.

VICTOR: What sort of shit are you talking, Da? I've told her I'll stop drinking. It's up to her.

BERT: She doesn't believe you.

VICTOR: So who's fault's that? If the silly bitch doesn't understand plain bloody English, what am I supposed to do?

BERT: Well, she's divorcing you – now if you're sincere you'll find a way of stopping her.

VICTOR: I'll go round and blow her bloody head off. That'll stop her.

BERT: It could also hinder the reconciliation.

VICTOR: I don't like you trying to be funny, Da. You're not very funny.

81

BERT: I'm not at my best at three o'clock in the morning.

VICTOR: I want her back, Da.

BERT: You'll have to talk to her about that – and she'll take a lot of convincing if you turn up like that.

VICTOR: (*Angry*) Stop being so fucking self-righteous. (*Pause.*) Sorry, I didn't mean to swear. You could help me. She listens to you.

BERT: She listens to what I say – but that doesn't stop her thinking for herself.

VICTOR: But you could tell her I'm going to change. You could tell her I'll stop drinking . . . tell her . . .

BERT: (*Cutting in*) Victor, you're always saying you're going to stop drinking, but you always have to be drunk before you say it. It makes other people a little wary. Just stop drinking, then go and talk to Jenny – when she can see the change for herself.

VICTOR: It'll be too late by then. We'll be bloody divorced.

BERT: Well, you can remarry her.

VICTOR: Are you right in the head? Do you think I'd make that mistake again?

(*Pause.*)

BERT: Victor, I'm 68 years old. Whatever sleep I need at night, I need it all in a lump. Come on and I'll make you up a bed, then we can talk again in the morning.

VICTOR: She'd love that, eh? Keep me here, sleeping, just to talk about her. (*Rising*) I've a woman waiting for me.

BERT: You're in no fit state to drive.

VICTOR: I don't have to be in a fit state – I'm a policeman.

BERT: I wasn't thinking so much of you being stopped by the police. I was worrying more that you might run them down.

VICTOR: I don't live here any more. It's not your worry now. I've got a woman to think of me now. You should meet her sometime. I can still pull a good bird. I'm not like Sam.

BERT: Why don't you let me call you a taxi?

VICTOR: (*Going to the door*) Call me what you like – I'm going home.

The Donaghy house. Early morning. THERESA *is sitting sipping a
cup of tea.* JOAN *enters, in her dressing-gown.*

JOAN: Did you go to bed at all last night?

THERESA: I woke up early and couldn't get back over. Those
    birds make an awful racket in the mornings. There might
    be a cup of tea in the pot – the light's not long out.

JOAN: I'll get some later. (*Pause.*) Mum, I'm going up to see
    Deirdre. I'm going to go to England with her.

THERESA: You're going to do what?

JOAN: I'll go back to work. She could maybe get a wee part-time
    job. Between us we could manage.

THERESA: I see – and me? I'd just be left here, like an old boot?

JOAN: You and Bert might get together again.

THERESA: You and your sister made a good job of ensuring that
    that won't happen. Now, having driven him away, you're
    planning to leave me on my own. A fine pair, I must say.

JOAN: You could come with us.

THERESA: Over to thon pagan hole? I'd look sick at my age. For
    the few years that may be remaining to me, I'll stay with
    Peter. (*Pause.*) I'd rather die here, amongst my own.

JOAN: For goodness sake, Mum. You're always on about
    dying . . . having picnics in graveyards. There's more to
    life than that.

THERESA: And there's more to it than going to England as a
    geriatric babysitter. I'm all right where I am.

JOAN: Are you not going to see him again?

THERESA: Just let the whole matter drop, Joan.

JOAN: I can't. I feel responsible.

THERESA: You are – but if that's the worst you ever do to me,
    I'll not complain.

JOAN: Didn't you love him?

THERESA: Love! Huh, there's so little you can do with it at our
    ages, it's easy to imagine it.

JOAN: You haven't imagined not being able to sleep.

THERESA: Woman dear, but you're a dreadful persistent person. Just leave me to look out for myself.

JOAN: You could write him a letter. If he replied that would be two for your shoebox.

THERESA: For the bit further I'm going, there's enough in the shoebox.

JOAN: Did you get the other one smoothed out?

THERESA: I burned it. (JOAN *looks at her*.) Sure, what use was it?

JOAN: You could have kept it – it's not as if it was taking up any room. (*Pause*.) I think I liked him. He was easy to talk to. The sort of man you felt you could trust secrets with.

THERESA: What secrets do you have?

JOAN: Well, if I had any.

THERESA: Your sister certainly trusted him with hers.

JOAN: I think you'd be mad not to see him again.

THERESA: He'll hardly want to see me, after that one's mouthful.

JOAN: Naturally he'd react like that at first. Who wouldn't? When he sits down and thinks about it, though, what does it matter? You didn't do anything wrong. Joe's away for life, so he's no threat to Bert's son. (*Pause*.) I'd just like you either to go back with him, or come away with us.

THERESA: You'll discover life's not just made up of the things you'd like. I'll be all right. Will you go back to nursing?

JOAN: I'll have no difficulty getting into a hospital over there. They never have enough nurses.

THERESA: How will you cope – with corpses and things?

JOAN: I'll manage. I have to face up to it again sometime.

THERESA: I shouldn't have burned the letter, should I? Funny, I half expected him to send me another one.

JOAN: He'll hardly do that. After all, you didn't respond to the last one. If you had . . .

THERESA: We all make mistakes. That's just the way it is.

JOAN: (*Looking at her*) Mum, the night our Peter . . .
    (THERESA *looks at her*.)
    Nothing. It doesn't matter.

The cemetery. THERESA *is sitting on the bench.* VICTOR *approaches from behind her.*

THERESA: Hello, Victor. How are you?

VICTOR: Fine. I thought I might have caught my da here.

THERESA: No, he hasn't been here today.

VICTOR: I thought you two came here every day?

THERESA: I haven't seen your father for a while.

VICTOR: (*With a laugh*) Did you have a row? Even at your ages, with time not on your sides? (*Pause.*) Join the club.
   (*He sits.*)

THERESA: Have you fallen out with him too?

VICTOR: Not with my da. I don't think so anyway. We fall out that often I'm never quite sure when we're on speaking terms and when we're not. It's the wife this time.

THERESA: I thought that was pretty much a permanent fall-out.

VICTOR: She's decided she wants a divorce.

THERESA: Don't you want it?

VICTOR: It's really none of your business.

THERESA: No, you're right.
   (*Pause. He glances at her.*)

VICTOR: I'm living with someone else at the moment.

THERESA: Well, you're all right then.

VICTOR: I don't want a divorce, and the bitch had no right to go ahead without even asking me.
   (*Pause.*)

THERESA: Maybe she's only trying to shake you up a bit.

VICTOR: Huh, she must fancy herself. (*Pause.*) I just think divorce is stupid.

THERESA: Your father's very fond of her.

VICTOR: He'd be very fond of anybody who was divorcing me.

THERESA: Did you ever try a reconciliation? (*He just glares at her.*)

VICTOR: So, will you and my da get married, or just live together?

THERESA: We don't have any plans to do anything. We're just sitting back watching the antics of selfish children we thought had grown up.

VICTOR: (*Quickly*) It's quite pleasant in here, isn't it?

THERESA: It is, on this side of the soil.

VICTOR: Maybe it's even better on the other side.

THERESA: That's silly talk for a young man. We'll all find that out someday. There's no need to rush it.

VICTOR: Whereabouts is your son buried?

THERESA: Just on the other side of the path from your brother.

VICTOR: I haven't been up here since the day of his funeral. No. I was – a mate who was shot a while ago.

THERESA: It must be very distressing when that happens.

VICTOR: It is, especially if you know the wife or family as well. You feel you should keep visiting, but there's nothing to say after the first visit. It's embarrassing. I never bother now. Bury them and forget them – and don't expect any more when it's your own turn.

THERESA: I haven't been up here every day myself recently. (*Pause.*) I suppose it'll not be that long before I am here every day though, whether I want to be or not.

VICTOR: I wouldn't want all this. I'd prefer to be cremated – no mess. Nobody has to worry about looking after a grave – and it's cheaper.

(*She looks at him.*)

THERESA: Where would you like your ashes scattered?

VICTOR: I'd like them put in a sandbag – then I could go on fighting the bastards. (*Realizing*) Sorry, I wasn't getting at you.

THERESA: I know you weren't. I wouldn't be one of the ones you'd be fighting.

VICTOR: (*With a smirk*) I've heard about you – the innocent. (*She looks at him.*)

THERESA: Will you have your father cremated?

VICTOR: If he wants to be.

THERESA: He doesn't. He wants to be buried here.

VICTOR: Well, then he'll be buried here.

THERESA: Even though it's more trouble – and more expensive?

VICTOR: I suppose the old bollocks told you I'd deny him the price of a decent burial. He's a great opinion of me.

THERESA: It's the opinion you give him.

VICTOR: If I thought he'd know about it, I'd build him a bloody pyramid – just to annoy him through eternity.
(THERESA *laughs and touches his hand with hers, unthinkingly, but in a friendly way. Realizing she pulls it away and looks at him. He looks at her and they both smile and give each other's hand a quick squeeze.*)

THERESA: You know, you're not really a bad lad if you'd let yourself alone.
(*They laugh.*)

VICTOR: Maybe her and me'll be friends, after the divorce.

THERESA: It happens . . . sometimes. It's easier when two people are free.

VICTOR: Ah, she's a funny bitch.
(*Pause.* DEIRDRE *comes along.* THERESA *is taken aback. These are the very last two people she wanted to see together.*)

DEIRDRE: (*Stopping and taking in* VICTOR) Have you lowered the age limit, Ma?

THERESA: Huh, fancy you turning up here. Deirdre . . . (*To* VICTOR) This is Deirdre, my daughter. This is Victor.

DEIRDRE: (*As they shake hands and greet each other*) Victor, as in winner over rivals, or is it a name?

VICTOR: (*Whilst* THERESA *sees her worst fears materialize*) As in a name. Victor Andrews. Your mother and my father are friends.

DEIRDRE: (*Taken aback*) Oh, that Victor. I mean . . . yes . . . you're a policeman?

VICTOR: 'Fraid so – but just Victor at the moment. Sit down. Here. (*She sits between* THERESA *and him.*)

DEIRDRE: It's nice here.

VICTOR: I was just saying that to your mother. Very pleasant. Her and my father spend a lot of time here. They have picnics.

DEIRDRE: Why not? It's the dead centre, isn't it? (*Silence.*) My brother's buried up here somewhere – but of course yours is too.

VICTOR: Just beside each other.

DEIRDRE: What a coincidence. (*Pause.*) I've never been up here before. I've never seen his grave. I'm not into graves.

VICTOR: Let's hope it's a long time before you are.

DEIRDRE: What? Oh . . . (*Laughs.*) Yes. I'm afraid the liking for these places hasn't been passed down. It is nice though.

VICTOR: I'm going to have a look at my brother's grave. Would you care to stroll across with me?

DEIRDRE: (*Rising as he does*) Yes. Why not? A police escort. (THERESA *crosses herself as they walk away and looks skywards. She gazes after them, shaking her head in silent disbelief.*)

JOAN *and* DEIRDRE *together, laughing.*

JOAN: I don't believe you – and are you going to go?

DEIRDRE: Why not? I've nothing to lose. I wouldn't dream of doing it, if we weren't going away – him a policeman and all.

JOAN: Do you see you . . . Is he good looking?

DEIRDRE: (*Screwing up her face thinking*) Rugged. (*Laughter.*) There was just something about him I liked. We told each other corny jokes.

JOAN: Does mum know you're going out with him?

DEIRDRE: She does not – and for goodness sake don't you utter a word. I'm just using it as practice – so's I'll know what to do when we get to England.

JOAN: Mum'll be all right here, won't she?

DEIRDRE: Of course she will. Quit worrying. She'll probably have Bert in before we're right out of Belfast Lough.

JOAN: I'd rather fly.

DEIRDRE: So would I – but I'm not that kind of bird.

JOAN: Keep your corny jokes for him. (*Pause.*) What did you think of the grave?

DEIRDRE: ???

JOAN: I mean, it's nice, isn't it?

DEIRDRE: For Christ's sake, Joan, I'm forgetting graves and martyrs. And through Victor Andrews I'm going to screw the RUC.

JOAN: Deirdre, that's disgusting talk.

DEIRDRE: It was intended metaphorically – if that's the same as waiting till you're asked.

JOAN: You're the end, you really are. Listen though, don't do anything foolish, will you?

DEIRDRE: Going out with him's not a very good start for that.

JOAN: Do you not feel a bit guilty though? I mean, your brother murdered, your husband in gaol – and you going out with a policeman?

DEIRDRE: It feels a little odd – but I couldn't think of any good reason, apart from those, for not going.

JOAN: Are you not frightened? Suppose they booby-trap his car – or shoot at it, and you there? What are people going to think?

DEIRDRE: You're too much like our da, Joan. Do you remember he used to always insist that he'd never go to San Francisco – because of the earthquake? I mean nobody ever asked him to go, and he'd never any plans to go, but he insisted he wouldn't anyway.

JOAN: I don't think it's quite the same thing. You are going out with him, aren't you?

DEIRDRE: I told you. He asked me, I said yes.

JOAN: So when do you actually see him?

DEIRDRE: Next Thursday, half-seven.

JOAN: Next Thursday! Deirdre, you fool. We go away next Wednesday.

(DEIRDRE *just looks at her for a moment, and they both explode laughing.*)

BERT *and* THERESA. *The scene is set in their respective living rooms. Each is reading letters from the other.*

BERT: 'They're fine. The children are thriving. They promise they'll send photographs in the next letter. They both write too. I knew Joan would, but I'm surprised at Deirdre. Sometimes her letters are the longest. If anything I think she's the one who's a wee bit homesick. "Look after yourself, Ma . . . keep well happed up . . . make sure you've plenty of coal in!" I could laugh at her. I'm going to need another shoebox at this rate.'

THERESA: 'You've my letters as well. Do you know I'm quite enjoying it – writing. It's a good way to pass the winter nights. I buy a wee pad every week in the post office when I go for my pension and a couple of stamps. That's the old army training – keeping the supplies topped up. I think it will be a long winter. It's been bad enough so far, but we usually get the worst of it after Christmas. If it snows I never travel far.'

BERT: 'I keep your letters by themselves – in the big Milk Tray box you bought me. You're lucky to have Jenny to look after you. I'm glad Victor calls for lunch sometimes. I can just picture that big brute arriving with his bunch of flowers for Jenny and his cowboy book for you – big spenders the peelers – but I suppose it's the thought that counts. Deirdre always asks about him in her letters. "How's the nice big policeman?" That was the strangest thing ever, and then her forgetting. It's not as if she was going to England every week. It just shows you, the good Lord's not as big a fool as we think. God forgive me for saying it.'

THERESA: 'I think if I die in the winter I'll get cremated. I know I'll not feel it, but it'll spare others from hanging around a cold grave and maybe it snowing on them. Victor says they can always bury the ashes in the grave, in an urn or a box. I know what you'll think but there's a great change in him. I think he'll soon be getting serious about this woman. Although I don't suppose you can get much more serious than living with someone seven days a week. He always asks about Deirdre too, and it's a bigger mystery to me how he got it mixed up. He's been playing snooker every Thursday night for years. Even when he's on duty, he's up to all the dodges of the day to get to it. I do hope you'll come and spend Christmas with us. Jenny's really looking forward to having you.'

BERT: 'I'll see about Christmas. I'd love to meet Jenny, but I've never spent it out of my own house before – away from my own hearth. You know I had to laugh to myself the other day. I heard someone on the radio talking about couples staying together for the sake of the children. I thought to myself, we stayed apart for the sake of ours! Now you watch that cold – you don't want it settling on your chest. Keep well happed up and take something for it. I don't want to be sitting on my own on that bench when the good weather comes in.'

THERESA: 'Jenny's looking after me a treat. Don't you fret, I'll take good care. As soon as the weather changes, nothing will keep me from that bench.'